ROBERT J STEPHENS

1

FIRST CONTACT

XHOSETI

Books also by this author:

XHOSETI - AD 2492

XHOSETI - MOON

FIRST CONTACT

ROBERT J STEPHENS XHOSETI FIRST CONTACT

3

XHOSETI

Copyright Robert John Stephens

ID 710955486088

FIRST CONTACT

ROBERT J STEPHENS

For my father, who sowed the seeds for this book a long... long time ago!

FIRST CONTACT

XHOSETI

"A pipe gives a wise man time to think and a fool something to stick in his mouth!"- C.S. Lewis

FIRST CONTACT

ROBERT J STEPHENS

EARTH

AD 2492

FIRST CONTACT

Chapter One

AD 2492
Earth
Atlantis Pyramid

Chris Stormburg woke up on the floor dazed, disorientated and numb.

Slowly, as feeling returned to his extremities, so did the memories.

There had been a humming noise, a flash and then some strange sensation, a kind of vibrating tingling, no...more of a pulsating sensation. He had felt the pulsating sensation deep down in his bones. The memory of it chattered his teeth as he shuddered at his inability to even morph a protection shield against the alien like onslaught.

What was he doing here...?

Where was here...?

Why was it dark?...Apart, that is, for , the faint glow of the crystals on the walls, or were they panels?

Then his centuries of conflict management training kicked in.

Groaning, he rolled onto his side and slowly, from a foetal position, managed to get on to his hands and knees. Now resting on all four extremities he fought

8

back a wave of nausea that very nearly overwhelmed him.

"Deep breaths...
One...
Two...
Three...
Ok...Get up!
Get on with it!"

Slowly he got to his feet, banging his elbow on what felt like a chair or table.

Feeling his way around he made his way towards one of the glowing panels; then he remembered his *Morph Suit,*

"LIGHTS!"

The suit morphed a few projectile shaped rods out of his shoulder blades which curved upwards and then, when horizontally opposed to each other, blazed brightly, lighting up the vast open space in which he had just awoken. Ten metres in front of him was a large rectangular block shaped console.

On the console a large red button flashed angrily.

"So they're here!"

He slapped his hand down hard onto the flashing button.

Everything lit up, bright pulsating waves of energy radiated throughout the room. He started to experience a similar excruciating pain as the vibration started all over again. Then, before he could command his suit to shield him from the bone shattering sonic attack, darkness enveloped him, and he collapsed to the floor, twitching and writhing in agony...

*

FIRST

CONTACT

Chapter Two

40000 BC

"This is the fourth planet from this solar system's sun, we must find something this time," thought Jorge.

"Soon this desolate solar system will be mapped and documented...just like all the others. No sentient life forms found so far, but...wait look at the readout!" he exclaimed, reading the ships electronic crystal display on his consol, *"Wow!* What a wealth of resources for us to mine, looks like we finally hit the mother lode," Jorge said to his right-hand man, number two in command, Sergio.

Jorge and Sergio had been chartered by the Galactic Mining House *UNMINE* to survey the planetary solar systems for new mining resources and any other form of exploitable wealth.

The drilling platform in the cargo hold had been bought and paid for by *UNMINE* but the transport Solar Planetary Skimmer, or *SPS* as they called it, was owned by him and Sergio, a *fifty/fifty* split. Everything split straight down the middle so there could be no petty squabbling over any of the profits from what they discovered.

Jorge ordered the onboard computer to survey the planet below, just as he had done on countless other

12

unremarkable planets in so many other unremarkable solar systems.

Not expecting much, the report appeared on the screen in front of him.

The planet's atmospheric composition report appeared on the screen:

Oxygen Level 18%

Nitrogen Level 70%

Hydrogen Level 0.05%

Helium Level 0.05%

Sulphur Level 0.05%

Chlorine Level 0.05%

Argon Level 3%

CO_2 Level 2%

Methane level 5%

Other 1.8%

Average day-light temperature: forty degrees Celsius.

Average night-time temperature: minus five degrees Celsius.

Gravity 91% of *SPS* current gravity.

Capability of human survival unaided 25%.

Morph Suits required? *YES*

"Well that cuts out having a picnic hey Sergio; do we need a more detailed atmospheric analysis?"

13

Sergio raised his head from the report on his screen.

"No, but I definitely don't think we will be able to have a picnic ether! But break out the shovels; I haven't seen levels of iron ore and precious metals as high as this anywhere else in the last five solar systems that we've surveyed!"

"Guess our new morph suits will cover the atmospheric issues though!" said Jorge.

"Planetary gravity looks good; the suits will adjust our densities to compensate."

Sergio continued, "Looks like there are pockets of methane gas being vented from deep inside the planet's surface. It must be coming from those tunnels that we can see on the surface. Suggest we head down and take a closer look," said Sergio returning his gaze to the computer screen.

"According to the surface scanners there doesn't appear to be any life forms on this planet, but who knows, *they* have been *wrong* before!" Sergio stated eyes fixed on the screen in front of him.

"No kidding Serg! Remember the last solar system we surveyed. The scanners picked up sentient life. It turned out to be intelligent algae, maybe self aware a million years from now, but really? Maybe we should adjust the setting on those *damn things, exclude*

14

anything that hasn't invented the wheel yet!" exclaimed Jorge.

"Most of the surface appears to be sand and desert, not much vegetation or water is being detected," continued Sergio unperturbed by Jorge's comments.

"Maybe the surest sign of intelligent life down there is that it's *hiding* from us. *HA...HA...*" laughed Jorge.

*

These new suits were incredible! They were semi transparent with what appeared to be faint blue and red arteries running through the suit. The wearer would quite literally walk naked into the suit and it would mould with the occupants' skin, giving a faint bluish tinge to the wearer.

This suit had a direct link to the occupant's cortex giving them unparalleled connectivity to any external stimulus or any actions the wearer wished the suit to perform.

In order to make one heavier the suit would simply absorb the required gas or liquid combination and compress as necessary, forming for instance, water sacks. These were created by the suit as needed and located in various positions around the body. The absorbed nutrients would be used to suit the wearer's

15

needs as dictated to it by the external environment they were in.

These sacks of water could even be used to hydrate the occupant by being directly absorbed into the blood stream via microscopic filaments that the *Morph-Suit* inserted into the occupant. The same would occur for any nutritional requirements the occupant desired or needed. Should the occupant require nutrition, all the wearer needed to do was touch the nutritious object. This would be absorbed by the suit and if not already broken down into a suitable absorbable molecular size, would be stored in a similar sack and broken down later.

When it came to any atmospheric requirements the environment was filtered through the suit's facial membrane so that only the right combination of gasses entered the occupant's lungs. Any toxic elements were automatically filtered out.

It could even extract liquids and gasses stored in the blood stream to ensure the occupant did not asphyxiate should they be in an environment without extractable breathing materials. This was unfortunately limited by what could be extracted from the wearer before becoming detrimental to the occupant's health.

If the wearer was required to lift any heavy object or exert themselves in any way, the suit could change

16

its structure with carbon like cellulose *nanotube* reinforcement in microseconds. The morph suit would then use the now modified hydraulic tubes as energy cells. The wearer would become as strong as any hydraulically articulated machine.

As far as safety and protection was concerned, all the wearer had to do was project the thought '*Shield*' and instantaneously a protective barrier would form where the perceived threat would strike.

The capabilities of the suit's shape changing ability were still undergoing testing but potentially anything the wearer can imagine the suit can conjure. There were limits of course to what shapes could be achieved, but that would surely change in future versions of the suit.

Advancement and new technology were happening all the time.

*

With their fifth edition suits, issued just weeks ago, the power source, always a downfall, had been replaced with two micro non-radioactive fusion driven power cells.

One would be used to power the suit whilst the run-down power unit recharged itself using the kinetic motion technology available at the time.

17

Each suit required this technology to be continually upgraded and modified. This was the weak point in this marvel of technical engineering.

The new suits take advantage of the wearer's heat signature and thermally activated motion sensors along the lines embedded in the suit. Every motion the wearer performs recharges the suit's power supply via the kinetic energy created.

When it came to modifying the wearer's breathable gasses in hostile environments, there had been, how does one put it, certain failings of the suit that had been detrimental to the *Morph Suit's occupant*!

Unfortunately, the previous versions of the suit had, under certain circumstances, managed to drain all the users' bodily fluids.

When the malfunctioned suits were recovered only an emaciated dehydrated husk of the once living occupant remained!

The new suits though, were guaranteed with an automated failsafe. In the unlikely event that a failure occurred, the corporation which had bought the suit could get a *full refund!*

Very comforting to the unfortunate emaciated occupant!

*

Exiting the Lander, now safely encapsulated in their morph suits, both Jorge and Sergio were standing close to one of the tunnel entrances they had discovered from orbit.

The tunnels were about two meters in diameter and seemed to be lined with a dark rubber like substance. Every three meters or so a ridge ringed the tunnel; something like the oesophagus of any creature that was required to ingest its food.

"Looks like we're going down into the belly of a beast!" joked Jorge.

"Still, no life signs showing on my heads-up display!

Whatever made these tunnels is long gone now!" projected Sergio to Jorge's morph suit.

"Still it's really creepy!" responded Jorge with the mind link.

"Come on, let's get on with it!

Down we go!" With that the two men walked into the tunnel.

*

After twenty minutes, the tunnel came to a huge open cavernous space; it too seemed to be lined with the same rubbery substance.

"Lights!" voiced Jorge, still getting used to the mental link with his suit.

19

Both suits lit up the cavern. It must have been eight hundred meters in diameter.
Hanging from the ceiling was a round ball, its surface also coated with the same rubbery substance. As they were looking at the sphere their lights reflected off a black tip forming on the bottom of the ball.

When they focused the suits' lights on the base of the sphere the darkness seemed to change colour. It went from obsidian black to a lighter shade of black then faded to grey.

This change of colour started to spread from the tip and then around the entire sphere. Within minutes the sphere had started to become transparent. The two men watched in wonder as the sphere changed into a bulging round sac which changed shape intermittently. Inside the sac there was a slight stabbing movement which increased in frequency until the sac throbbed and pulsated.

Looking on with fascination, Jorge and Sergio were transfixed beneath the once inert sphere.

"Are you getting this? Is it a new organic life form? The first we've encountered in ten solar systems! My sensors are not showing that it's a carbon-based life form though! It's more silicon-based and the *methane* levels are increasing *rapidly!*" reported Jorge.

"*Damn! There goes our monopoly on the mining rights!*" cursed Sergio.

20

"Let's hope they aren't *greedy!*" Jorge commented, the excitement visible in his wild gestures.

"Jorge, I'm getting a bad feeling about this!

I'm going to head back up the tunnel! If they aren't friendly at least I'll have a head start! I mean, it looks like they have been in hibernation for quite some time and I'm sure they must be hungry," said Sergio, concern evident in his voice.

"Come on Sergio, they're not even carbon based, we probably wouldn't even be on their menu. This could be an historic *first contact!* Who knows, I'll probably get a statue in some city that we create on this desert planet! I mean wow, just think of the *possibilities!*"

Then the sac burst!

Ten half a metre-long *insectoid* like *alien* creatures spilled out and down onto the waiting Jorge.

"SHIELD!" screamed Jorge.

The suit reacted immediately as the six-legged creatures swarmed over him, their intentions clear.

Here was an energy source...

"Welcome...Welcome! We are the Xhoseti!" a voice screeched inside his head. The Insect like creatures started to bite and claw at Jorge hungry for his flesh.

21

The suit was resistant to the scraping and biting of these insectoid jaws.

The Morph-Suit shielding held firm!

Jorge tried to stand but his legs were swept from under him. Crashing to the ground and in a panic, Jorge swung his arm toward his attackers, a blade now extended from the tip of his hand. The suit had projected Jorge's weapon of choice for him to defend himself, acting almost pre-cognitively.

The morph blade he had summoned glanced harmlessly off the attacker's chitin like armoured exoskeleton as he flailed around wildly.

Having failed to break into the suit, the swarming aliens released an acid-based compound from a gland under their mandibles and engulfed Jorge with it.

At first the suit shrugged off the new chemical attacks, but this was a new untested version of the *Morph-Suit* and part of their assignment was to test the suit to determine its limitations.

The suit, having determined that more resources were required to overcome the increase in toxic gases and fluid on Jorge's face covering, started to extract the required nutrients from his body.

Jorge felt himself becoming weaker as the suit drained his body of the required fluids to enable him to inhale.

22

Then the failsafe kicked in, the suit shut down all external defences determining that breathable air was of more importance than external shielding. It then redirected all available resources to that task.

*

Sensing the change in Jorge's suit and subsequent armour, the *Xhoseti attacked again!*

This time the new energy source screamed as they amputated and dissolved its extremities.

One by one Jorge's amputated arms were dissolved in the acid released from the *Xhoseti*'s gland sacs. Soon all that was left of his bones and flesh was a steaming pile of red gel lying on the floor.

Each *Xhoseti* projected a proboscis like attachment from its head and began sucking up the pile of liquid-like-flesh that had once belonged to Jorge.

The first *Xhoseti* to exit the sphere stood up on its hind legs and made a clicking noise.

All activity ceased. The rest of the *Xhoseti* scurried back and formed a circle around Jorge.

The leader released a sharp pointed probe from the base of its abdomen and approached the groaning human, stinger at the ready.

Stabbing Jorge in the stomach it expelled a batch of eggs into his abdomen. Jorge screamed and fell paralysed to the floor.

23

XHOSETI

The *Xhoseti* continued to feed on him, removing his legs one by one; then, using another gland under their mandibles, sealed up the wounds with a dark rubbery excretion.

They intended to keep the new resource alive for many more eggs to come.

*

Sergio, having witnessed the ferocity of the attack on Jorge and then seeing the *Xhoseti* swarm all over him, had hoped that the suit would protect Jorge.

Then seeing the mark five morph suit fail, Sergio turned and ran up the tunnel as fast as the suit could propel him. He heard Jorge's screams and that gave new speed to his exertions.

The suit was now registering the new life forms; eleven in all; Jorge was still alive! Sergio tried not to imagine what they were doing to him.

Two of the *Xhoseti* raced up the tunnel chasing down the other new energy source. It was quick, but they were gaining...

Soon they would be upon it and more eggs could be laid. They had been in stasis for so long, but now was the time to be revived and to start rebuilding their civilisation once again. This carbon-based life form was the key to their revival.

Sergio had reached the tunnel exit.

24

FIRST CONTACT

Luckily, they had set the Lander down within fifty metres of the entrance. Still to cover that fifty meters seemed to take an eternity.

Sergio screamed for the Lander to open the hatch. It took a full ten seconds to open, during which he could hear the scratching and clicking of whatever it was that was chasing him.

He dived into the Lander bay and screamed for the hatch to close. Another ten seconds passed before the hatch had closed and sealed. *Why was it taking so long!*

"Thank You...Thank You!" blurted Sergio. *It* was then that he heard the clicking noise behind him.

"SHIELD!" he screamed. The suit took the impact of the blow from the unwelcome *Xhoseti* stowaway.

The repeated blows to the suit were like watching an insect in a glass beaker realising it was trapped and trying to get out, except in reverse. He was in the beaker looking out whilst the creature was trying to get in...

Gathering his wits, he issued a command to the Lander's computer,

"IMMOBILISE INTRUDER, THEN FREEZE FOR STASIS AND TRANSPORTATION."

The *Xhoseti* invader froze under the liquid nitrogen spray. *Still alive*, its many faceted eyes tracked his

25

every movement even though it could not turn its head.

A pod appeared and the *Xhoseti* was enveloped into the manifested hibernation sac.

"That's that! Now who's the prey hey?" thought Sergio.

The council would want a full report, and who knows, he may even get that statue that Jorge wanted so badly, especially with a living sample in the hold.

Sergio trained the Lander's external defences on the remaining *Xhoseti* which was trying to gnaw its way into the cargo bay.

There was a bright light as the laser made contact with the intended victim and then the internal gases of the creature must have ignited as a bright explosion engulfed the creature.

Its head and limbs were scattered all over the desert floor making satisfying plunking sounds as some of the body parts hit the Landers's hull.

Shaking with relief, he instructed the Lander to lift-off and when in range dock with the *SPS* in orbit.

Man was he glad to get off that nightmarish ball of sand and rock.

"Let the council deal with those evil murdering Xhoseti!"

*

A GALAXY
FAR AWAY

FIRST CONTACT

Chapter Three

33000 BC
Space
Vicinity of Planet Termite

Graham had been training hard, graduating in the top five percent of the navy's space marines. He had received his wings yesterday along with the rest of the graduates. Man, was he ready to take on those alien invaders! When the time came he would be ready.

No-one knows how or even why the war began.

That was thousands of years ago!

All he knew was that when he had woken from his growth pod he felt like he was born for the job!

Graham had the physical attributes of a twenty-five-year-old human male. Standing five-foot eight inches, he is of medium muscular build, sporting brown eyes and dark thick hair. All his muscles were fully developed, being both lean and strong as if he had been in constant training from an early age.

The academy training took only six weeks to complete thanks to his enhanced genetic physical and mental prowess.

The amount of food needed to be consumed was the biggest issue. Five thousand calories of drooling green slop three times a day. All the human body needed to grow and develop in such a short period.

Now fully trained and ready for active duty Graham was to report to his *battle cruiser*.

*

Graham was more than capable of using the many forms of weapons available to him in the weapons locker. Although he had not physically held any of the weapons, he knew that should he need to pick up and fire any of them he would have no problem in doing so; in fact, he knew he would excel in their use.

His *DNA* had been modified to allow his muscle memory to react as if he had used them for the entire twenty-five years that his body knew it was.

"A T T E N T I O N!

CAPTAIN ON DECK" barked the Boson.

As one, the freshly graduated space marines stood to attention, the click of marine boot heels hitting each other in unison.

"Stand easy men," ordered the Captain, pausing before continuing,

"As you know we are at war with the *Xhoseti*. Every thirty-three years we gather our forces at the same

29

location and time, to kick the living shit out of each other." The Captain paused again for effect,

"There is rarely a victor!
Generally, all men and ships are destroyed on both sides, the flagships on either side being the only vessels left intact! So, have no doubt in your minds that you are going to die!

All we can do is hope that we have one more missile, one more ship, one more good man, one such man who can react that fraction of a second quicker than the enemy," the Captain took a deep breath.

"WILL YOU BE THAT MAN?"

As one the space marines replied,
"YES SIR...YES SIR!"

The hatchlings have turned out better this time; they are more of a cohesive unit. Hopefully this time the battle will be different.

He has given that same speech hundreds of times. His longevity was mainly due to the restorative powers of his *All Terrain Skimmer* or *ATS* assigned to each of the ship's captains.

Each Captain of a vessel entered the *ATS* of his battle cruiser and used it as a command and control

30

centre, effectively controlling his men and weapons via genetically imprinted code. The men and women under his command were just drones that he controlled with his thoughts. He doubted that the result would be any different to any of the previous battles though. For every enhancement they make the *Xhoseti* have one of their own.

"What would it take?

How will mankind overcome this adversary?

There appears to be no end to this war with the Xhoseti!"

*

The fleet had gathered at the usual place in space. Originally the site had been chosen for the barren wasteland that it is. There was quite literally nothing here in this part of space; no planets, no asteroids or rocks, *not even a speck of dust!*

The remains of the previous battles have been completely removed and recycled to make each conflict more efficient.

Resources being as limited as they are, every scrap of building material, organic or otherwise, was collected for recycling.

Not only are the ship materials collected and reused but all the cadavers as well.

Nothing could be wasted!

31

Once the desiccated bodies had been collected, they were sent to the *Resyk* centre where the remnant nutrients remaining in the cadavers were used to repair existing soldiers or to re-grow additional soldiers. The un-repairable bodies were gathered up and ground down to be used as part of the nutrition requirements for those being reformed in the growth pods. The dead soldiers would make up most of the slop the newly hatched marines would consume during their six weeks of training, with of course the required vegetables and nutrients; hence the green colour.

*

Admiral Holste surveyed the approaching *Xhoseti* fleet.

How many times had he been here, a hundred, maybe more? *The first battle was just a slaughter!*

The *Xhoseti* approached claiming peaceful intentions and requesting a meeting.

It was a trap; nearly all of his fleet had been destroyed!

The automatic defence grids on his ships had returned fire and destroyed almost as many *Xhoseti* ships as *they* had destroyed Human ships.

Three Xhoseti destroyers made it through to the planet's defence grid; luckily, they were destroyed

32

before causing too much damage to the colonised *human* planet *Termite*.

Only the *ATS* had saved his life, ejecting him from his cruiser and taking him back to the planet under the protection of an invisibility cloak. He had to spend a few days re-growing his left arm in the regeneration vat. Every now and then he still feels the twinges of the old arm as if he had two left arms instead of one; he wasn't sure which one was causing the itching.

"No more surprises!" the Admiral made a mental note.

The Xhoseti are out to destroy all those who compete with them for the galaxy's resources.

"It's succumb and be consumed, or fight and die, or just possibly, survive. Well, we will not go into the night without a fight!" thought the Admiral defiantly.

As normal, there is *no warning*.

Lights flash on the bows of the *Xhoseti* destroyers as weapons fire and missiles were released. His fleet reacted as normal with the automatic defence grid.

"Here we go again!" said the Admiral, fear and excitement evident in his voice.

*

Space marine Graham is part of a boarding team heading for the closest *Xhoseti* destroyer.

Geared with a limited version of the *Morph-Suit* and zero recoil phase pistol, he stands in his drop pod and waits. He is not nervous; this is what he has been *bred for!*

For some reason, he knows that the pistol will not be his weapon of choice. He taps his eight-inch serrated laser edged knife. Feeling the light weight blade comforts him.

There is a huge tearing, tortured sound as the light dartlike craft spears itself into the skin of the *Xhoseti* target.

The drop pod cocoon sac ensures that none of the marines are injured. If they were then ramming the *Xhoseti* ship would have been a pointless exercise.

Then it's out and into the enemy ship. Pulling his pistol, he fires upon the *insectoid* like creatures that are spilling into the corridor where Graham and his fellow marines are waiting.

His orders are clear, kill as many of them as possible.

Life is not important!
Only victory!
Rising from behind his cover, he mentally projects:
"MORPH, SHIELD"

34

A *Xhoseti* warrior raises a blaster and fires a range of different projectiles at him; he spins and weaves as he runs toward the insect like creature, his own pistol firing.

The laser blasts merely deflect off the scale-like armour the *Xhoseti* is wearing. Not so with the projectiles fired from the *Xhoseti* weapon. A round of heat hits him in the chest. Then another of extreme cold!

He feels his *Morph-Suit* begin to disintegrate where the *slugs* have impacted his chest.
Nearly upon the enemy, Graham pulls out his laser edged blade and slashes at the *alien creature*. The blade slices through the *Xhoseti* armour. There is a screeching squeal from the insectoid as one of its six limbs is sliced clean off.

The *Xhoseti* grabs hold of Graham's left arm and tries to yank it off. Luckily for him he still has the blade in his right hand and with a curving downward slash, he starts removing the *Xhoseti*'s extremities one at a time.

Just when the insectoid looked like it was about to take its last breath, front mandibles reached out from its mouth and grabbed hold of Graham drawing him into the creature's mouth.

The *Morph-Suit* has died and is of no use in protecting his face against the *Xhoseti*'s attack. Using his laser blade, he drives it into the neck of the *Xhoseti*

35

warrior severing the head from its body but it's too late!

Grahams face is now nothing more than a mess of tendons and sinew, bones and flesh dissolved away in the regurgitated acid attack that emanated from the creature's gland sacs.

Both man and insectoid fall to the floor dead!

*

Surveying the battle, which has proceeded in a similar manner to the last one, Admiral Holste scratched his heavy beard.

"Another stalemate!" spat the Admiral.
As usual, only his flagship and that of the *Xhoseti* command remain.

It is time to start the cleanup and regeneration process. What a waste!

So now the cycle starts all over again. With that he mentally starts to issue commands, relaying back yet again another battle, another stalemate.

"The council will not be pleased!" he muttered under his breath.

Then let's hope they have another plan because who knows what will happen when either our, or the *Xhoseti*'s, resources eventually run out!

*

ROBERT J STEPHENS

PROJECT

EARTH

FIRST CONTACT

Chapter Four

32000 BC:
Termite

"*Krys* Reenberg!"

"*I've summoned you here as a matter of the utmost urgency!* I will explain," said the *Grand Master.*

Krys, having proceeded to the main office of the Planetary Consortium as per the message he had received, was standing in a large conference room facing the *Grand Master*; no one else was present.

"As the Grand Master for the Council of the Galactic Planetary Consortium, it is time to enlighten you as to our current position in the ten-thousand-year war with the *Xhoseti*.

Believe me, there are far worthier men to take on this mission but, as it was your genetic ancestor who devised the project, so it would appear that you are the right man for the job!

As you know we are...at best, in a stalemate with the Xhoseti!

Resources are nearly depleted on both sides.

It will only take a slight edge by either side to completely annihilate the other.

We fear that mankind will not be the victor.

Even if we do succeed in winning this colossal war, we will be fragmented and without resources for many hundreds, if not thousands of years.

This will in turn result in our already depleted genetic pool being diluted even further!" the *Grand Master* paused to take a breath, then continued,

"Extermination of humanity will be but a prolonged inevitability. As such we have had in place for some time now a contingency plan, *'Plan B' if you will!*

Approximately forty thousand years ago, one of your ancestors devised a long-term social experiment involving the seven tribes from the various human occupied planets.

Certain genetically selected men and women were chosen for mind-wipe and hyper-stasis pod transport to a planet at the furthest edges of the galaxy. It took some twelve thousand years for them to reach their destination which appeared to be ripe for colonisation.

I believe it is called Earth!

Each tribe was set down on the planet as geographically remote from each other as possible and allowed to develop unimpeded by the *Guardians* who were there only to monitor their progress. The only genetic programming that was installed in each tribe's *DNA* was the desire to worship a deity, belong to a sect and to strive to build step-pyramids at certain co-

39

ordinates, the plans of which are genetically coded into their *DNA*.

As a side effect of the building of the pyramids we are hoping that the seven tribes will succeed in joining mankind in one common purpose and as such eliminate the infighting that so plagues our species." Stopping again to take a sip of water the *Grand Master* continued,

"If we weren't so intent on survival against the *Xhoseti* we would be consuming our resources to kill each other, this being the true nature of the human race.

This will be the end of mankind unless we find a way to live together, not in harmony of course, but at least not at war! That will have to do in the beginning.

Three of the pyramids, as a failsafe, will be constructed by the *Guardians* and be made of a composite of plastic impregnated stone material so they can last the many thousands of years required before, if all goes to plan, they are needed.

These three pyramids will be submerged in the seas of the planet Earth. The co-ordinates of where they are to be placed will be revealed to you in due course.

Only your *DNA* will be able to open the portals into the pyramids and use any of the technology that we send with you.

You, or your descendants, will be the only humans with the correct *DNA* to activate the planet's defences which are to be hidden inside the respective seven pyramids."

Krys waited patiently for the part of the *Grand Master's* monologue that entailed his involvement. "What we require of you is to travel to the planet Earth and ensure that all is proceeding as required with regards to the construction of the defence weapon system. The only way to fire the defence weapon system, once complete, will be to have each of the seven tribes in a mind link. The mind link will be used to create a planet wide mental projection. This too is implanted in their *DNA*.

When the time is right you, or your genetic offspring, will activate the seven pyramids. Silence will descend on the people of planet Earth and the *DNA* coded instruction will be activated.

The weapon will be fired, closing the worm hole created by the alignment of planets in that solar system."

The *Grand Master* projected an image of a *Xhoseti* warrior into *Krys's* mind.

"We presume that the wormhole will be controlled by the *Xhoseti* approximately thirty-two thousand years from now.

41

It is imperative that the wormhole be closed preventing the *Xhoseti* from entering the Earth's solar system. Failure is not an option as it would mean the end of all mankind both here and on Earth.

Krys, do you have any questions?" asked the *Grand Master*.

"Well of course I have a few thousand questions, but firstly how do I survive the *twenty thousand* years once I arrive at Earth?"

"We are sending an *All Terrain Skimmer* with you that is capable of morphing into any shape you can project with you mind. It can also traverse sky, sea, land and space.

The *ATS* has an unlimited energy source as far as we know. Where that energy comes from we do not know though. The *ATS* will be activated by your *DNA* and body heat. It will also contain an embryonic regeneration sac to revitalise and maintain your body during the many millennia to come. This regeneration sac will however not sustain you indefinitely.

You will need to find a suitable mate through whom you can pass on your genetic *DNA* code. This child will need to continue your work of uniting humanity in the construction of the pyramid weapons and the uniting of mankind both politically and religiously.

You will also be required to impart your knowledge and technical knowhow to your offspring. They in turn

42

will be required to do the same should it be required. This will be accomplished via the *ATS*.

Ten generations should be sufficient to take you to the point of survival or destruction of the human race.

That is when we have predicted the *Xhoseti* will arrive. Please also bear in mind that if you and your offspring succeed, the *Xhoseti* will be exhausted and you may choose to exterminate them or embrace them.

The choice is yours! This we have foreseen."

The *Grand Master* continued, "Remember we want to end the cycle of destruction, not perpetuate it."

"Well thank you for the information, but how will my genetic memory remain stable and be transferred to my offspring?" queried *Krys*.

The *Grand Master* paused for a moment and seemed to be in communication with someone not present in the room.

"We will imprint your memories on each of your genetic offspring that enters the *ATS*. It is imperative that each generation enter the *ATS* to be assimilated prior to the age of four Earth years. Any later and the mind link memories will not be seamlessly transferred to your newly formed apprentice."

Mind whirling with vivid and horrifying images of the *ATS* eating and regurgitating his child gave him a shiver up his spine.

"*Krys... Do* you accept your assignment?" asked the *Grand Master*.

After a slight pause, "Yes, *Grand Master*, I will take the assignment."

"*Good!*" said the *Grand Master*, "Now follow me."

Krys was led into a brightly lit chamber and instructed to sit in a large black chair.

An oesophagus like tube snaked its way towards him and attached itself to his temple. There was a smell of ozone and electricity then a feeling of euphoria accompanied the faint humming sensation that he felt when the snake like tube sank its probes into his brain.

"That sensation you are feeling is the probe projecting feelings of wellbeing into your cortex.

This is required as the actual sensation of copying your *DNA* imprint, then coding all the technology and access panels to you is extremely painful. For reasons you do not need to know we need you to be conscious during the procedure," explained the Grand Master.

"When complete you will be rendered unconscious and should awaken twelve thousand years from now in orbit over Earth.

Good luck! The fate of mankind rests with you should we fall in our fight here!"

Krys was left with the humming machinery, his imagination predicting only the very worst.

FJRST CONTACT

"What a burden to be handed, the fate of mankind in my hands, wow!" thought *Krys*.

No matter what the circumstances though, he would of course have accepted this great honour and the chance to save mankind.

"I may even get a statue of myself somewhere in the Universe!"

That was of course if he was successful!

As soon as the *DNA* process had completed, *Krys* sank into a deep sleep. His body was transported to the stasis pod and his biomechanical *ATS* ship ready to blast off for Earth.

*

EARTH

Chapter Five

20000 BC:
Earth Orbit:

Krys opened his eyes; a soft blue light radiated from the environment making him squint as the glare hurt his unused eyes.

He can hear a soft humming sound; then the memories start to come flooding back to him.

"Where am I?"

Moving his head slowly, *Krys* looked around the small cocoon that he had awoken in. The sac was glowing with various light and dark pulsating red and blue veins on the encapsulating *ATS's* walls.

Then he remembered...

So that is what the pressure was on his chest; he was still in the embryonic sac. Mentally *Krys* gathered his strength and issued a command to the *ATS*,

"EXPEL!"

"Unable to comply" replied the *ATS* in his head.

"Countdown to 'Expel' in three thousand seven hundred and twenty-three seconds," continued the whisper.

He waited, mentally reviewing the immense responsibility he had been entrusted with.

"How was he ever going to achieve such an impossible task?"

47

He waited patiently.

"Expel in three...two...one." the *ATS* informed him.

There was a humming noise and *Krys* was standing on the floor next to his All Terrain Skimmer completely naked. He looked at the craft, a liquid like shimmering cylindrical vessel.

As he placed his hand on the shimmering surface, a whisper in his mind queried,

"Entry?"

Krys pulled his hand away.

Looking around the room that he had been placed in, *Krys* noticed some panels not too far away.

First things first...food and drink!

Walking up to one of the glowing panels, he placed his hands palm up under the ledge of the panel and then stretched out his hands. Somehow, he knew exactly what to do next.

"NOURISHMENT," *Krys* commanded of the panel.

Two small balls appeared in his palms, one blue and one grey. He popped them one at a time, blue first, into his mouth and swallowed.

They each had a slimy coating.

He started to feel them slowly expand in his shrunken stomach. The nerves in his abdomen sent sharp shooting pain signals to his brain from the stretching of his stomach pouch but quickly subsided. The coating on the balls must have had an anaesthetic

48

chemical in it; soon he started to feel sated although slightly light headed.

He felt full and slightly sleepy, strange that after being in hibernation for twelve thousand years he should want to sleep.

Still, the chemical reaction he was experiencing just showed how human his physiology really was. Only then did *Krys* realise that he was stark naked.

"What to do about clothing?"

A voice in his head whispered,

"Think and it shall be so,"

"Grey *apparel...Mirror*" said *Krys.*

Krys stared back at himself in the newly formed mirror.

The person staring back at him had long wavy white hair, white medium length beard, piercing grey eyes that shone slightly and a long grey gown.

"Hmm...not what I imagined, but a good start!"

Just as he was reviewing his new image he heard a hiss behind him. An opening appeared behind him and seven black clad hominid figures with stern angular features entered the room. Their appearance seems out of proportion, huge heads resting on tubular shaped bodies. The heads making up approximately two fifths of the peculiarly shaped form, they look human, but barely so.

"Greetings Krys Reenberg," a voice in his head whispered.

"We are the *Guardians*, our task is to manufacture and place the three-fail-safe step-pyramids of Atlantis, Easter Island and Japan.

We are also to observe the progress of humanity with regards to the construction of the remaining four pyramids.

We are only to observe social, philosophical and religious progress of the seven tribes that were sent to Earth. Those areas of influence are entirely your domain. We will render any help should you specifically request it. You are however cautioned to use these requests sparingly and wisely.
Any questions you have will be answered and relayed to you via the mind link in your *ATS*."

After a slight pause the *Guardian* continued, "We advise you to start your assignment by observing the warring factions on Earth. Humanity, true to form is trying to destroy itself as per normal. After your observations, we would appreciate a report and proposed plan of action.

You may decide to wait in stasis until the time is ripe for you to sow the seeds of tolerance and well being to all of mankind."

With that monologue the *Guardians* as, one turned and left the room.

"Ok!" thought *Krys*, *"On with the show."*

Turning to his *ATS* he placed his hands on the ship and mentally projected,

"Entry"

A tube-like appendage appeared out of the *ATS*, enveloped *Krys* and swallowed him back into the embryonic sac deep in the bowels of the strange bio-mechanical craft.

This was strictly a one-man vessel.

An appendage attached itself to his temple.

"Earth, take me there!"

Krys felt a strange sensation, like silk rubbing on his skin. The *ATS* moved away from the orbiting *Guardian's* station, slowly at first, and then proceeded to speed up.

Within moments they were flying through the Earth's atmosphere at incredible speed. Only the cushioning effect of the embryonic sac protecting *Krys* from the gravitational forces generated.

"Cloak...

Go lower...maintain five hundred meters above grade elevation.

Find local tribes,"

Within minutes *Krys* was staring at a village somewhere over central Africa.

The village below was on fire and there were men and women scattered about on the ground most dead, some in the throes of death.

A group of men, presumably the invading force are taking turns in raping a small girl possibly pre-teenage.

"Zoom in..."

Her face had a glazed look about it,

"Zoom eyes..."

She was already dead.

One of the attackers pulled out a blade and hacked off her foot which he proceeded to bite into and tear off bloody red chunks of flesh.

"NORTH...Take me North," Krys mentally projected to the *ATS*.

The *ATS* flew on until they found a cave in Southern Europe. The cave had wisps of smoke emanating from the entrance. All seemed peaceful as the wind blew the smoke eastward, bending the tree tops slightly.

Nothing but the wind rustling the leaves could be heard, not even a bird tweeted.

"Land...

Expel"

Standing next to the *ATS* Krys mentally instructed to himself,

"Cloak."

The *Morph-Suit* obeyed his command.

Krys appeared to shimmer and then faded into the environment.

To the casual observer he had simply disappeared. Walking towards the cave *Krys* heard movement coming from the entrance.

Two cave dwellers dressed in animal skins and carrying spears appeared. He walked past them into the cave and heard a low groaning noise accompanied by some grunting from somewhere towards the back of the cave. A fire was burning in a shallowly dug pit that was surrounded by mismatched large stones; a humanoid leg was hanging in the smoke rising from the damp fire, being cured for future consumption.

Krys then noticed human eyes flashing just behind the fire.

Two captives, both Neanderthals, were hanging from some crudely made rope tied off on an overhanging rock.

One is missing a leg and appears to be barely alive; the slashed joint has been tied off with a leather thong to stem the flow of blood.

Sickened, *Krys* turned and left the same way he had entered.

*

Back in the *ATS* he took a moment to compose himself, then thought,

"West...

Take me to Britain."

Villages with reed roofs appear below the *ATS*. Clusters of huts, sometimes as many as ten grouped together around a larger central hut are scattered over the grassy landscape. Everywhere else is thick wooded forest full of wildlife.

There are people covered in animal skins doing everyday chores, tending fires, nursing children, gathering fruit and seeds from the nearby land.

Wait, a group of men and women are gathering around an elderly bearded man with a walking stick.

He is dressed as a...? The *ATS* in his mind prompts, *"Druid!"*

They are listening intently to what he has to say.

"Observe conversation...Translate" *Krys* requested.

"People of lower England, you must respect the ways of the land! Mother is the earth and the water. Father is the sky, the stars and the sun. Only take what you need from Mother and leave the rest to replenish," the Druid was telling his gathered flock.

"There will be a feast at the Wooden Circle at the time of the summer solstice. Bring all to welcome Father as he joins with Mother to renew the seasons. We must celebrate their union as the new season is

54

conceived." There was a cheer from the gathered villagers. The men, eager to revel in the festival of copulation and intoxication, roared their approval. The women's response was just as enthusiastic.

With the knowledge that the villagers will ensure the festival would be a success, the Druid turned and walked back into the woods, presumably to find the next village.

Krys, having seen enough issues his next command, *"Mexico...*
Take me there..."

Time and space seem as one...

*

Krys looked down over the heavy jungle which teemed with arachnids, reptiles and birds of all colours, shapes and sizes; the jungle thrived with wildlife.

A bounty of what Mother has to offer.

They hovered over a sleeping village; only the calls from the jungle disturb the slumber of the inhabitants.

Slowly...creeping as stealthily as would a jaguar on the hunt; a band of men approach the sleeping village.

In an act of planned co-ordination, the band quickly went about setting the primitive jungle dwellings alight. With the flammable buildings set alight, the band of

55

men hid, lying in wait for the inhabitants to wake from the smell of their burning huts.

Panic ensues!

By the time the villagers realised what was happening...it was too late.

Panicked and scared, the villagers ran from the burning huts only to be ensnared in rope traps set strategically around the village. Once subdued and bound, the captives were taken to a nearby village in a clearing that was three days walk away.

There they were paraded in front of a man with brightly coloured bird feathers set about his torso. He selected a few of the captives to be separated from the others. The bound captives are subdued with a club to the back of the head and then the bird man proceeded to cut off their extremities one by one. He then, having inflicted as much suffering as possible, decapitates the unfortunate victims one by one putting them out of their agony.

The ground was soaked with the blood of the slain.

Krys, seeing yet another example of man's cruelty decides to move on.

"Japan...

"Take me there!"

There is a hum and again that silky sensation.

Time and space appear to be one...

*

56

The village he now hovers above has a familiar layout, round reed covered Rondavels are scattered in an organised pattern around a central larger hut. This village radiates a feeling of calm and tranquillity. As he travels the island similar villages litter the landscape, conflict appears to be nonexistent.

It would appear that being isolated on a small island...as long as there were sufficient resources to provide for all, reduced conflict to a minimum.

Man will always have strife; that is Mother's way.

After all, no animal will willingly allow itself, or its offspring, to be eaten to feed another.

Without strife, complacency would set in and progress would be stifled. His report would reflect that.

For now, at this moment in time, there is not much to work with and *Krys* feels that to instil any unity towards deities or sects will be diluted by the conflicts he has observed on most of the habitable planet's surface.

Disease and famine in the centuries to come will decimate mankind further; there was nothing to work with, he would have to wait.

In the *ATS* he sends his report back to the *Guardians*.

"Your conclusion and plan of action?" came the response almost immediately.

57

"I have none!" then returning his attention to the
ATS,
*"Take me to Earth's highest mountain,
Find us a cave...
Conceal us..."*

Time and space seemed as one...

Soon the ATS had reached central Europe.

"Stasis?" questioned the *ATS.*

"Yes...

Awaken me in five thousand years,

Stasi...Now..."

With that *Krys* dropped into hibernation to await an
era when mankind will have become more civilised. Let
the *Guardians* guide man through this *time of
savagery!*
He knows that if mankind continues down this path
of destruction and violence they are all doomed.
The *Xhoseti* will enjoy turning man from predator
to prey!

*

58

FIRST CONTACT

INVASION

FIRST CONTACT

Chapter Six

18000 BC:

Earth

Southern Europe

Ureg and Oek were walking through the forest below the snow-capped mountains. They have been camped in the cave midway up the side of the cliff for the winter. The river below is good for snaring fish and small animals.

Today though, there was a smell in the air that seemed unfamiliar.

The smell of wet burning wood touches the air; it reminds Ureg of the horrific events of the previous summer. Recently though there have been signs of other hunters in the forest. A few discarded bones of the larger animals, even the remains of the biggest bear they had ever seen.

Normally they would be running away and climbing the trees to get away from any bears in this part of the forest, especially when a mother bear had cubs with her and was looking to fatten them up. The berries only provide so much nutrition for those great beasts.

*

Today, the forest seemed restless, there was a new apex predator on the roam and even the bears are in hiding.

Ureg sniffs the air, catching the scent of something unfamiliar. While wondering what this new scent was his mind wandered to the memory of when he had a mate. Her long ginger coloured hair always gave him such pleasure when he stroked it.

There were many of them then, all living in a small encampment down by the river.

He had had a son, also with ginger hair, which surprised him as his dark hair was thick and coarse like his father and mothers.

His boy was nearly ten summers of age almost fully grown and ready to help them with the hunt.

His mother had been teaching him where to find the roots and fruits that they would eat with the animals he snared...*Then one day it happened!*

They came in the night, fire on sticks, these new invaders from across the river.

They also had sticks with stone blades fixed into them; one of the little girls tried to run away and was cut down with a swift swing of one of the invaders weapons. The murdering man pulled out a piece of flint blade and cut the little girl's throat sealing her fate. He had just started to gut her like an animal when the leader, a particularly big man barked some strange sounding words at the butcher.

The murderer then stopped what he was doing and stood up, his scared face scowling in the glow of the burning sticks. They were very organised these new human hunters.

No orders needed to be issued, not even hand signals as they rounded up Ureg and his tribe into hastily constructed wood and rope like pens.

Then the invaders made a central fire with the fire sticks.

Ureg and the tribe were all scared; some of the females were sobbing, some weeping, some shrieking and bashing the ground with their fists.

These new men from the South all spoke a strange language that he had never heard before. There were more words to their language than he and his folk had ever heard, and most were unrecognisable.

The leader issued commands and the men obeyed; strangely some of the words were familiar to Ureg but he had never used them all in one seamless stream.

He could understand one or two of the words being spoken but not the intent of what the leader meant. Many times he had tried to remake the words that he could not understand but the way these new men clicked and moved their tongues made it impossible for him to repeat the sounds.

He and his people got by with actions and hand signals for the most part, a few words for danger or animal that they all understand. It had taken many years just to achieve this level of cooperation amongst the hunter group which was why they were so successful at surviving.

When it was time to mate, the female normally approached the male and in a brief encounter a child was made. Besides silence was a much better way of stalking game, the less noise the better.

These new people were taller than he and the rest of the tribe. Even the women stood half a head above him!

In the morning though, their intentions became clear, his brothers were taken and strung up by their arms in a few nearby trees.

The females were taken off into the forest. What became of them he did not know, but the noises and screams coming from the forest would indicate to him that there was consensual or forced mating taking place. As long as the females survive then that was all he could wish for them. Maybe they will be taken into this new tribe and be fed and sheltered, not killed like the little one.

Later he found out the fate of the rest of the little ones. He had awoken to the rising morning sun heating his face when he saw the scarred man stoking the

63

central fire. More wood was added and a few of the new men were standing around the fire passing a leather bag from one to the other. Before passing it to the next man, the holder would take a long drink from the bag.

With each drink from the bag the men seemed to become more and more unstable, staggering into each other and using their comrades to hold one another up. The more they drank the more their voices changed until Ureg could no longer make out any of the words he had previously recognised.

A fight broke out and soon the big leader man came to see what the commotion was about.

Over his shoulder was slung a little male, one of Ureg's brother's offspring. From the way the little male was hanging from the big man's shoulder he was clearly deceased. Tossing the dead child to the men he barked some orders.

The fighting stopped and the scarred faced man from the previous night pulled out his flint blade once again and started to gut the child dumping the child's internal organs into the burning fire.

Soon there was the smell of burning flesh rendered in with the sizzle of fat falling onto the hot coals.

All Ureg and the other tied up captives could do was look on in horror as this grizzly feast unfolded before them.

It was not unknown for his folk to eat the dead just to survive when the big ice had taken the land, and everything froze, but this was different. That was a long time ago but was part of a nearly forgotten shameful folklore that was handed down from generation to generation in the hope that it would never happen again. The hand paintings in the caves tell of that dreadful time when all the animals and plants died. Survival makes folk do evil extreme things.

It was all that they could do to survive!

Even so, most of those who could not trek south or break the ice to hunt for fish, perished.

Now this on the other hand; to actively hunt his people and eat them was beyond his comprehension.

Ureg resolved to escape.

Turning to Oek, he started to make his signals and words that they both understood.

Later, when the invaders had eaten and drunk their fill, one by one they fell asleep.

There was only one that remained awake, the one with the *scarred face!*

He walked up to Ureg, poking him with his flint blade, drawing blood every now and then and grinning into Ureg's contorted face.

Even though Scarface hadn't consumed as much as the others he was still a bit unsteady from his participation in the grizzly feast. While he was taunting

65

Ureg, Oek managed to kick Scarface in the back of the knees putting him off balance. Lurching forward to stop himself from falling, the scarred faced man fell face first towards Ureg. As he fell Ureg raised his knees straight into the man's face. His head snapped backwards and there was a loud cracking noise as scar-face slumped to the ground, his neck twisted at an unnatural angle.

The flint blade that Scarface had been using to torment Ureg had fallen out of his hand when his neck snapped and was lying next to Oek's feet.

Partly luck, partly sheer desperation, Oek managed to grab the blade between his toes. The sharp blade bit into his flesh and blood trickled down his digits and onto the ground.

Swinging his legs, he managed to get his foot on Ureg's shoulder and pulled Ureg carefully towards himself. He wrapped his left leg in between Ureg's neck and raised arm.

Using the blade clutched between his toes, he began the slow painful process of cutting the rope.

Soon...both were free.

Ureg took the blade and moved to cut the other four captives free. They were gesturing and calling loudly to be released from their bonds. Ureg put his finger to his lips to signal for them to be quiet but it was too late.

With all the commotion, a few of the slumbering men around the fire started to stir.

Ureg cut the bonds of the first captive and then gave him the invaders bladed stick.

One of the invaders sat up, rubbed his eyes and shouted something that sounded like the word Ureg used for danger. The now alert man grabbed at the others next to him waking first one then the rest.

Ureg grabbed Oek and pulled him towards the direction of the forest. As they entered the edge of the forest he turned to see what had become of the rest of his folk.

Weakened from being tied up for so long many of them had no defence against the blows from the invading men, blood and screams filled the air.

Without hesitation he and Oek ran as fast as they could away from the camp. Using all their tracking and hunting skills they eventually arrived at the river. Seeing that water skin pots they used for fishing were still tethered to their respective trees they climbed into them and floated down the river.

Ureg started to contemplate what they were going to do next.

First hide, find a cave next, and make a pointed stick for hunting and protection, then find some food.

Life it seems was going to be a lot tougher now with the new human threat from the South.

67

Next his main goal would be to avoid these new foreign men and head North in search of any of his fellow brethren in the hope of shelter and to find a way to retaliate against this new threat from the South!

*

ROBERT J STEPHENS

EGYPT

69

FIRST CONTACT

Chapter Seven

10000 BC:
Earth
Egypt

Krys opened his eyes.
A bright blue light filled the embryonic sac; even in the protective fluid he could feel the shudders and tremors running through the shell of the *ATS*.

He requested a report and environment external view.

"Landslide!"

A portion of the mountain had disappeared and the *ATS,* although cloaked, was hovering one hundred meters above the nearest mountain surface. Snow swirled around the cylindrical shape of the *ATS,*

"Take us down...

Land...

What year is it?" projected *Krys* to the *ATS*.

"10000BC," tickled the whisper in his head.

"Why have I been in stasis five thousand years longer than I instructed?"

"The Guardians have been monitoring and guiding the development of the seven tribes and felt that not

70

enough progress towards change has occurred to warrant reviving you from hibernation," responded the *ATS.*

"So...things have changed?" questioned *Krys.*

"Potential exists for indoctrination
Populations have banded together and are in need of instruction. They look for leadership and have the thirst for religious instruction.

Sects have been formed." the *ATS* responded in his mind.

"Where is the highest level of civilisation?"

"Egypt." whispered the voice in his head.

"Nourishment, I need food and water..." said *Krys.*

A *feeling* of warmth filled his mind along with a tingling sensation in his bowels. Memories of happiness and wellbeing flooded his mind.

Feeling sated, he returned to the task at hand.

"EGYPT,

Take me there,"

That silky sensation again, space and time seem as one...

*

Krys and the *ATS* were submerged in the Nile River...close to the city of Giza. The *ATS* is still cloaked and awaiting *Krys's* next command.

71

"Morph...
Nile crocodile,"

The largest crocodile ever to roam the Earth formed from the *ATS's* shell with *Krys* still inside it,
"De-cloak,
Make landfall,"
Pausing a moment...*Krys* took some time to think about his next move,
"Walk to the closest settlement west of current location."

*

Imotep was barely twelve summers old and as such he had been sent to the Nile to draw water to slake the thirst of the herd of cows his father was tending to.

Life continues as the Nile dictates.

She floods, she moves, she silts and migrates about the delta as a snake follows the scent of a prey. It has been so for thousands of years.

Later his father will sacrifice a cow to Ra, the sun god. The blood of the cow will be used to entice the return of Luna the Moon goddess and the cycle of life for the next year will continue.

Then he saw the largest crocodile he has ever seen emerging from the Nile's river bank.

Frozen in his tracks he lay down on his belly, prostrating himself before what must surely be the god of the Nile.

The massive creature looked at him; grey eyes shimmer as it lumbers past him towards the settlement in the West.

Shaken and trembling Imotep rose to his feet and ran off to find his father.

*

The *ATS* approached the settlement; people are screaming and running away.

This was not the reception that *Krys* was trying to achieve.

"Cloak"

The ATS shimmered and vanished.

"Expel"

Krys was standing on the outskirts of the settlement, his white hair whisking in the hot breeze.

A small boy ran towards him,

"Mister...Mister...be careful there is a great river beast close by, come away...come with me!"

The boy grabbed *Kry's* hand and led him into the town. The boy kept staring at him with a quizzical look.

"You have grey eyes, just like the Nile crocodile god I just saw! Where are you from stranger?"

73

"I am from the East little man. I must speak with your Pharaoh; will you take me to him?" *Krys* replied to the little boy.

Without speaking Imotep, still holding *Krys's* hand, led him through the town towards some large wooden gates guarding a great house.

"The Pharaoh is in there," pointed Imotep to the high wooden gates.

He let go of *Krys's* hand and ran back the way they had come. Soon the boy had vanished into the depths of the small city.

A pair of guards stood in front of the great gates barring his entrance. One of them seemed to be studying *Krys* with bemused interest.
Krys walked up to the lead guard on the left and projected a thought into his mind,

"I am a wise man from a great king in the East.

Take me to your Pharaoh*, I have important news that he will wish to hear. Pharaoh Tutenseti is expecting me.*

DO NOT KEEP YOUR KING WAITING!"

The guard issued a command to the guard on his left, presumably his second in command and the man opened the gate, ushering *Krys* inside.

*

74

Inside the building there is a stairwell and nothing else. *Krys* descended the six flights of stairs into a dimly lit chamber. In the flickering light of the oil lamp lit room, he could barely make out a throne in the middle of the chamber. On it sat a man with a golden head piece shaped in the form of a striking cobra. His head nodded sporadically as if he was in some kind of trance.

As *Krys* approached, Tutenseti raised his head and stared at *Krys* through hazy brown bloodshot eyes.

The effects of opium inhalation were clear to see.

To *Krys* the opportunity to make an impression couldn't be more obvious.

"Your highness, I come from the East and bring news of a majestic future for you and your kingdom.

All your subjects will go down in history as the creators of a *great new civilisation!*" *Krys* paused for effect.

Krys studied the Pharaoh to see if there was any acknowledgement of anything he has said; hoping that the drug induced fog could be penetrated.

"Who are you?" commanded Pharaoh Tutenseti.

"I represent the Grand Architect of the Universe and am here to offer you a great opportunity to lead your people in a quest that will save the entire world and humanity," replied *Krys.*

75

"Tell me more," whispered Tutenseti, his mind filled with images of power, conquest and vast wealth.

"*You* and *your* descendants will build a great step pyramid, the plans and designs of which will come to you in a dream.

You must gather the resources and manpower to build this wonder of a monument to your greatness.

As a precursor to the great pyramid that you are to build, it would be wise to apprentice and skill your work force on a lesser monument of some sort.

May I suggest some form of *lion*, maybe a..." *Krys* mentally commands,

"*Suit...Morph,*
Nubian Lion"

The air around *Krys* shimmered and an image of a Great Nubian Lion lay resting on the chamber floor snarling up at Tutenseti.

Tutenseti, still in his drug filled state flinched backward with a cry of horror.

The air shimmered again and *Krys* is standing in front of Tutenseti, white hair and beard glowing in the soft lamp light, his grey eyes flash.

"*Cloak*" and then he vanished.

Cloaked, *Krys* ascended the stairs until he was outside again,

"*ATS to me.*
Entry."

76

FIRST CONTACT

Once inside, *"Where* is the next highest level of civilisation?"

"Britain" the voice in his head whispered.

"Take me there!"

Time and space seem as one...

*

Tutenseti awoke from his drug filled slumber. What a strange dream, he really must cut back the use of that opium pipe. Was that real, the white-haired man and the lion?

Neverless, the vision of the great lion lingered in his mind. Recreating this vision in stone will show the world the greatness which lay in his blood.

"GUARDS!

Bring me the leader of the builders' guild...*NOW!"*

A short time later the head of the builders' guild was lying prostrate in front of Pharaoh Tutenseti.

From his prone position the guild leader cautiously spoke,

"Command me o king of Pharaohs," absolute obedience evident in the builder's trembling voice.

"You will build me a monument of a great Nubian lion with the head of a Pharaoh next to the Great Nile River. It must face the East to welcome the rising sun each day.

The Sphinx will symbolise the waking of a great nation with the rising of each day." commanded Pharaoh Tutenseti

Builder: "As you command my Pharaoh," and scurried out of the room to begin his greatest and most dangerous building project.

*

The air around the *ATS* shimmered and *Krys* stirred inside the embryonic sac of the biomechanical entity. The *ATS* was hovering, cloaked, above a small island on the West coast of Britain. Below is a large circular wooden building surrounded by a stone circle of megaliths.

"Where are we?" he projected to the *ATS*.

"Anglesey, home of the Druids...

They are the social and religious leaders of Britain." whispered the *ATS* in his mind.

As *Krys* observed the comings and goings of the villagers below, a young woman was walking towards a flat stone table on the eastern side of the stone circle. She does not struggle, is not bound and appears to be leading the procession.

Behind her follow women and men dressed in animal skins with wooden masks of mythical creatures carved and painted on them. A druid dressed in a white robe with a wreath made of oak leaves on his head is standing in front of the stone table holding a bronze sickle larger than a man's head.

The young woman strips naked and lies on the table exposing her throat.

When the young woman had settled on the stone sacrifice table the druid turned to address the gathered men and women.

Facing the East, he started to sing and chant. The crowd goes down on their knees and following his lead start to chant as well, swaying from side to side as they sing.

The woman on the stone table tenses, the druid sensing her unease turns to the naked young woman and utters some reassuring words.

She relaxes, and then lies back down on the stone table again, exposing her throat.

The bronze sickle comes down in a quick arch; her head falls from the sacrifice table and down to the ground.

Blood spurts from her arteries into a stone bowl at the foot of the table. The severed head is gathered up and placed on top of one of the megaliths shaped like a pregnant woman.

The ample stone shaped breasts that had been carved onto the megalith were meant to represent the mother of creation.

The decapitated sacrificial victim's body is gathered up by a few of the followers and placed on a funeral pyre.

The druid then walks up to the pyre and sets the wood alight. Smoke fills the air as the tar smoulders and then catches.

The men and women start to dance around the pyre, animal horn goblets full of fermented berry juice are drunk with enthusiasm. With the singing, cavorting and consumption of the alcoholic berry juice, it does not take long for the celebrations to end. Exhausted the revellers fall asleep almost as one in a circle around the now pile of ashes.

"*Land*" instructed *Krys*.

"*Expel*"

Krys walked towards the large building in the centre of the stone circle; no one stirs or challenges him.

Entering the circular wooden building *Krys* noticed that there is a stone stairwell at either end of the building.

Around the edges of the building are what looks like bed pods hanging from the building's walls. All are unoccupied as the revellers have all collapsed outside next to the remains of the sacrificed girl.

Reaching the eastern stairwell *Krys* entered the stairwell and descended into the bowels of Mother Earth.

80

The stairwell is lit by tar burning torches; the smoke makes his eyes burn and he instructs the *Morph-Suit* to filter the irritant away from his face. Reaching the bottom of the stairs, he looked around.

It appeared to be empty and only dimly lit by similar tar fuelled torches. On the walls flickering in the dim light are spiral art works. He stared at the largest of them.

Ten minutes later he roused from what would appear to have been a mesmerising trance. He felt a hand rest on his shoulder and then a voice beside his ear whispered,

"Why are you here brother?"

Startled, *Krys* turned to face the druid he had seen perform the sacrifice.

"I am here to bring news of an impending doom!" projected *Krys* to the druid.

"The fate of mankind lies in the hands of you and of those like you," responded *Krys* verbally to the man holding his shoulder.

After a pause the druid responded,

"Hmmm...a wise man needs a little time to digest news as strong as that! Come; let us rejuvenate our mortal bodies."

The druid then turned and walked to a portion of the room which looked as much like a solid wall as the

81

rest of the building's walls did. It too was covered in spiral art.

He reached out taking hold of the artwork and pulled it aside. Only then did *Krys* notice that it was a leather skin painted in a similar fashion to the walls.

Behind the skin facade was a small room with table and stools. This room too was dimly lit with burning tar torches.

The druid sat down at the table and a servant covered in spiral patterned paint placed a bowl of dried meat and fresh fruit in front of him and the druid.

The druid picked up one of the bowls and after taking a piece of stringy dried chicken, handed the bowl to *Krys* indicating for him to eat.

Even though he is not hungry, or for that matter worried about being able to digest the food, he ate. His internal organs have been genetically enhanced to handle any micro bacteria or disease that may be on planet Earth.

If he does not eat, he knows that it would raise suspicion and probably offend his host.

Having selected a piece of meat himself, the only sound in the room is that of mastication as they both devour the meat and then the fruit that has been provided.

Some beer is brought by the servant and when the druid has drunk his fill, he placed the horn, now drained of its contents on the table.

The druid wiped his mouth and let out a loud rasping belch and then proceeded to stare directly at *Krys*.

A few minutes pass until eventually the druid spoke,

"I have not seen you before in these parts," more a statement than a question.

"Strangers are viewed with suspicion here and may even be made an example of. For all I know you could be a spy from a hostile tribe?" the druid let the question hang in the air.

"That is true, I could be a spy, but I am not hostile.

I come from the East over the water. The one thing I can tell you is that I mean you and your people no malice. I have foreseen a great peril that will engulf all of mankind. The power to prevent its occurrence resides with us, the leaders of the land and sea. If we do nothing to prevent it, we will all perish!"

After a long silence the druid indicates to the spiral patterned servant to leave.

Without a word the painted man left the room.

"We are alone...Now you must convince me why I must help save the human race, and, if I am convinced, what I must do,"

Krys stood up and thought,

"Morph...

Tree Dryad"

There was a shimmer and now standing before the druid was a living tree.

"I am the representative of Mother Earth.

You will gather your people and form a Pagan cult. I do not require human sacrifice, but any other offerings will be accepted," *Krys* paused to gauge the druid's reaction. Seeing none he continued,

"You will live together in harmony only taking from Mother as you require.

You will gather all the men and women of Britain to build a circular monument of giant stones. This will be done with the aid of all the British tribes.

Each tribe is to bring hard stones from their native province to be placed in the stone circle.

This is my command!

Now sleep and it shall be as if I visited you in a dream."

With that *Krys* projected a low frequency sonic projection towards him and the druid fell to the floor unconscious.

"De-morph...

Cloak"

Krys left the room and headed back up the same stairs he had entered by.

"*Master*...master, are you alright?" asked the servant having returned to find the druid asleep on the floor.

The druid awoke, still groggy; he pulled the servant close and whispered in his ear,

"Help me outside...gather the people, I need disciples. We have much to do and many to influence." *Krys,* now back in the *ATS,*
"Well let's hope that the seed of civilisation has been sown. It's a small start but a start it is."

From organising these small tribes into larger groups of people with a purpose, sects will start to form, and religious organisation emerge, laws will be made, books may even start to be written. The fate of mankind hangs by a very...very fragile thread.

"Where to next?" asked *Krys.*

"The Guardians are recommending that you return to stasis.

They will wake you when civilisations are about to form or are in need of a push in the right social direction."

"Well then take me to the highest point on earth so we can hibernate."

The *ATS* shimmered, time and space appear to be one, that now familiar silky sensation engulfs *Krys.*

Krys looks around.

85

There is something familiar about the snow and mountain rocks below him.

"Hibernate.

Only awaken me in an emergency or on instruction from the Guardians."

Darkness envelops him as he sinks into the deep sleep of hibernation.

*

SAQQARA

EGYPT

Chapter Eight

5000 BC:
Earth
Egypt

Krys, feeling the need to return to Egypt, was certain it was time to check on the progress of the step-pyramid in Saqqara. Although he had sowed the seed with Pharaoh Tutenseti five thousand years ago prompting him to build the Great Sphinx, he presumed that there would be a great civilisation and religious order in place by now.

Laws and guilds will surely be of an advanced nature.

He hovers, cloaked, five hundred meters above the Great Sphinx to admire the craftsmanship of what has now lasted approximately four and a half thousand years.

A bit of wear and tear, but nothing that a bit of maintenance could not rectify.

The Pharaoh Tutenseti is still clearly distinguishable on top of the lion's body. The pyramid on the other hand appears to have made little or no progress. The base has been set out and the base building blocks placed, but it appears that any attempts to build higher than three plateaus have all but been thwarted.

Collapsed ramps littered the building site, the lower ones to the first and second plateaus were still intact, but the ramps to the third have collapsed; they were too steep.

It was time to intervene!

Krys landed the cloaked *ATS* close to the nearby town of Giza.

"Expel"

Krys found himself standing on the sandy desert just outside the town walls. Covering his head with a kufiya and then with the stoop of an old man made his way through the front gates and into Giza. When inside he stopped in the shade of a palm tree and took stock of his surroundings. There appears to be little to no activity.

What should have been a hustling and bustling construction town was indeed a quiet non-productive market town.

Krys decided to find the nearest tavern, which was probably the most active part of the town, even though it was still a few hours before noon.

Sitting down at a table in the corner of the tavern he started to listen to the locals complaining about their current overseer,

"*Imotep... bah!* That great waste of space calls himself the *great builder*...hmm, more like the *great*

89

failure. The Pharaoh will visit next week and will probably chop his head off.

Then where will we go? There is no work to be found and it's not like anywhere is hiring megalithic stone masons. I mean, it's not like it's a skilled job, just *bash...bash...bash* all day long, day-in...day-out. Heat the stone...add the water... smack the *donkey's ass. Ha!*

I suppose that's where the skill is. Don't hit the wretched donkey too hard or it won't put the wretched stone block onto the rollers." complained the drunken stone mason.

Tomb decorator: "I on the other hand, am still *waiting* to do my job! Last tomb I decorated *was three months go*!" slurred his bleary-eyed companion.

Krys got up from the bench he was sitting on, having overheard all he needed.

Walking over to the tavern inn keeper who was standing behind a simple wooden counter top, he put a golden arm band on the bar counter.

"Where do I find the *great builder* Imotep?" asked *Krys*.

The tavern owner quickly snatched the golden arm band and with a quick fluid movement it had disappeared into his grubby leather overcoat.

He then raised his head and smiled at *Krys*, stained teeth grinning from under the thick black moustache.

90

FIRST CONTACT

"Turn left on your way out, keep walking six blocks. It's the one with the red painted rooftop, can't miss it! Now get out of here before someone *notices you!*"

Grinning the inn keeper watched *Krys* leave, wondering how he was going to get more of that gold in his hand from the stranger that had just appeared like magic, putting his hand into his apron pocket,

"What the..." exclaimed the barkeep as he pulled out his hand which was covered in a thick gluey substance.

"Where is my gold band? HEY YOU...STOP!" but *Krys* had already left the building and cloaked.

Krys, now back in the near empty street, followed the instructions from the tavern owner and was soon lost.

"There is no straight up the street!

It's all twists and turns! Can't miss it, seems to be an *exaggeration* at best!"

He wandered around in circles, and then tired of retracing his steps; he mentally projected to the *ATS*,

"Find me a building close to my current location with a red roof top."

Moments later a map with the walking route was projected to his mind.

"I must have just missed it! Two lefts instead of a left and a right!"

Within minutes he was almost back where he had started from. *Krys* soon entered a large courtyard and to the northern side of the square was Imotep's large rectangular shaped double storey residence with a red roof.

Not in the mood for niceties he commanded the suit,

"Cloak!"

Banging on the wooden door he waited. A wooden hatch opened just at eye elevation and then slammed shut. A lower hatch opened and then it too was slammed shut.

Nothing happened but the sound of curses and mutterings about the Genies of the desert emanated from behind the closed door.

Krys banged again on the door, this time louder.

More curses could be heard from inside, then the door burst open and a guard rushed out sword drawn shouting,

"If this is a prank, I will gut and eat all the children I find, starting with you, Mustafa, you little bow-legged son of a camel merchant!"

Krys slipped past the irate guard and into the cool courtyard of what must be Imotep's residence.

The area he found himself in looked like Imotep's place of relaxation and contemplation. Water fountains spray mist into the plant filled garden. The

92

sound of running water fills the air immediately soothing one's troubles away. With his current building project a failure and with that his own impending doom, this cool garden courtyard would be the place to contemplate ones' final moments.

Krys de-cloaked and strode up to the bald-headed man that lay sprawled on his side.

Imotep's feet were dangling in the shallow pool located in the centre of the courtyard.

A gem encrusted silver goblet lay on its side having been recently knocked over. The remains of a wine amphora, now shattered, are all over the terracotta tiled floor.

"Someone threw a bit of tantrum!"

Krys called over a servant,

"Get some water and fruit for your master."

The servant soon returned with a bowl of fruit and a jar of water.

Krys took the water and poured it over the immobile body of the *great builder*.

With a sharp intake of breath Imotep roused and then with a rapid succession of quick gasps sat up.

Looking deliriously around Imotep shook his head; his blurry eyes flaring.

"Who dares to... to wake the Pharaoh's *great builder* with such disrespect?" croaked Imotep between cracked lips.

93

Krys projected into Imotep's mind images of downed tools, broken ramps and an incomplete pyramid.

"Are you the *great builder* that I seek?" asked *Krys*.

Imotep, still groggy from the previous days of constant wine consumption, shuddered.

He knows he is behind schedule and when the Pharaoh returns to check on the progress of the pyramid will have Imotep's head on a stick.

Not knowing who this stranger was, Imotep prostrates himself before *Krys*,

"The spies must have sent word of my failure and this is my assassin!" thought Imotep,

"May Horus have mercy on my soul! *Please be merciful*! Tell the Pharaoh I will double the work force! I will sacrifice more goats to Anubis and Ra, spare me and I will not fail him," pleaded Imotep.

"I am not here to take your head, rather to save it. *Get up and sober up!* Then I will need some papyrus, ink and a quill to write with. This is your lucky day!" replied *Krys*.

A few hours later Imotep, red eyed and still a bit groggy but now almost sober, joined *Krys* in the great study.

Imotep has been re-dressed by his servant and now holds his head high, a man who has achieved great things but now is willing to accept his fate.

94

Krys was just finishing the last touches to the parchment he has before him.

On it are some sketches of the step-pyramid, counting out the exact number and size of each stone per level.

Imotep comments that he has done a similar exercise and that this is not the problem,

"The transportation of the huge stones is taking too long. They keep sinking into the desert once they have been taken from the boats down by the Nile." explained Imotep.

Krys already has an answer ready for this problem.

Producing another sketch with the details of a flat-bottomed boat that could be used to skim across the surface of the desert sand.

"That is a great idea!" exclaimed Imotep.

"Like we use the water, we can use the sand!"

I will get men to make as many as are needed immediately.

We will pull them through the desert with camels! IBREHEM,

ATTEND ME!" shouted Imotep.

*

After Ibrehem had been sent away with the rudimentary sketch of the desert boat, Imotep turned to *Krys* and scratching his head,

95

"One problem down, many more to go," but the twinkle in his eyes had returned.

It was as if a condemned man standing on the gallows could now see that the hangman's noose has been poorly made and hope sprung from that slightly frayed knot.

Krys cleared his throat to speak,

"I have noted that ramps you have constructed are too steep Imotep. You will need to use no more than an angle of fifteen degrees to the horizon or a slope of one vertical to four horizontal when building the outer pyramid walls. Anymore than that and the sand for the desert boats will begin to slide down the ramps of their own accord. If the sand slips, the sand boats used for pulling the stone up the ramps will become useless. You must not let this happen."

Imotep called for another man servant, to whom he passes a hastily drawn sketch of a ramp filled with rubble. The rubble ramp was to have a covering approximately one meter deep of fine desert sand for the shallow sledges to glide over.

"Get those drunken scum out of the taverns and back to work! All of them, even the decorators!" commanded Imotep.

"Now they have orders, if I get the chop, they get the chop, *I am sure they will exceed all my expectations!*

96

If not, I will do the chopping myself!"

Krys: "Problem two solved. Now for the biggest issue, how to get the stones up the ramps?"

Imotep explained his problem,

"We have tried all manner of beasts and men to get the stone blocks up the ramps. When the elephants panic, they have gone on the rampage and killed many men. It was only the mahout's striking of his chisel though the elephants' brain that saved my own life on *one occasion!* We have lost so many elephants and men in the past few months I fear that they will not be replaced in time." moaned Imotep.

Placing his hands on his temples Imotep cradled his head feeling very sorry for himself.

"We are all doomed!" he sobbed.

"This is a bit trickier, but with the desert boats and the elephants used in a different manner I believe the stone blocks can be moved up the ramps.

Here is what I propose."

Krys explained to Imotep that once the stones are at the base of the ramps, a pulley system involving ropes and logs can be implemented.

"You will build a wooden tower stabilised at the base with heavy stones in the middle of each plateau. If a man sits on the top of the tower and he can just see the bottom of the ramp, then it is high enough.

You will place a large rounded log, with no sharp edges, on top of the tower. Make sure it is well secured.

Grease the top and sides of the log, then run a rope the size of a man's torso over it. This is to be attached to the desert boat on one end and on the other side attached to your beasts of burden or elephants in this case.

They will be on the downward ramp, so it will be easier for them to pull the flat boats. Then once they reach the desert floor they will not see what they are pulling. That should stop the beasts from panicking.

Make sure that all on the project, including the animals, are well fed and watered.

Now to organise the work force.

For the men, strict rations of beer, two tankards in the evening only, *no more!* Deal harshly with any who flaunt this rule.

You shall lay down greased logs of wood to slide the stones over and into place on each level. They shall be made immobile by chocking them in place.

Once at the top of the ramp, the desert boats are to be disconnected and the pulling ropes wrapped around the great stone being positioned." *Krys* paused to get his breath then continued,

"The stone itself is to be pulled onto the greased logs. Once in place, have your men disconnect the ropes and lever the stones into place.

Remember, grease or animal fat is the key here! Without it none of this will work. You will have to replace it on a regular basis for the sand will turn it into a cutting paste if you do not. Use sheep or pig fat, the men will need the protein for strength so use the meat to feed them."

"Do you have a sketch of what you are envisaging?" asked Imotep.

Krys pulled out a papyrus scroll from under his cloak and handed it to Imotep.

Krys has had some time to think about this crucial issue,

"This only solves the problem of laying the stones for each plateau which you will have to repeat over and over making the pyramid higher and higher.
Remember, when a man sits on the tower he must just be able to see the base of the ramp. You may have to build many ramps.

Do not exceed fifteen degrees or the one to four slope ratio and if needed make the ropes longer. This does not solve the method to be used in raising the stones for the inner chamber's construction though.

To solve this construction problem, you will also need to provide a system of pulley logs with smaller

99

offset pulleys above a central square stone tower. *Krys* drew a small sketch on a piece of papyrus detailing the layout of the pulley system to be used. You can use the pulleys to raise the inner stones to the top of the construction tower and then manipulate them sideways to be placed where needed. I propose allowing four access passageways at the base of the pyramid located North-South and East-West for raw material ingress. The stone blocks are to be pulled via the shallow boats to below the central pulley.

Then using the hoist ropes pulled up to the third highest level of the tower which must have access openings three blocks deep to thread the stone blocks through. Once in place attach ropes to pull the stone blocks sideways so they can be moved to where they are to be placed. All of this will need to be done using elephant power again. As the inner workings increase in height, so the constructions towers height will have to be modified. The finer details I will leave to you.

Eventually you will need to move the pulley system up to the top of the walls of the king's chamber to hoist the final blocks into position. Gravity will be your ally when you swing the blocks down the sides of the existing structure and slide them into their allotted positions. The actual manpower, beast power, rope and pulley design I leave in your capable hands."

100

One week later the Pharaoh arrived to check up on the progress of his pyramid.

The Pharaoh, suitably impressed, summoned Imotep.

Prostrate before his Pharaoh, Imotep awaits his fate.

The Pharaoh speaks:

"*Imotep...*It would appear my spies have misinformed me as to your lack of progress. I came here to put your head on a spike. Instead, being suitably impressed, I now come here to cover you with gold, and not the molten version that I have been preparing in your honour for the past three days. You know, the one that would have burnt you down to your bones. You have saved yourself, your family and all the workers you employ. Slave bring the gold coins!

Now cover this miracle pyramid builder in coins for he has pleased his Pharaoh greatly!"

*

Krys, cloaked and hovering above the Pharaoh's procession smiled.

He then projected his next destination to the *ATS*,

"*China...Plains of Xi'an to be precise! Find the closest town, Xianyang I believe it to be and take us there. There is a certain emperor Xiashian that needs a push in the right direction.*"

101

With that the *ATS* shimmered and that silky sensation encompassed him again, time and space appear to be one...

Krys looked down upon a large open field, a few buffalo it's only inhabitants.

*

ROBERT J STEPHENS

XIANYANG

CHINA

103

FIRST CONTACT

Chapter Nine

5000 BC:
Earth
China

Krys landed the cloaked *ATS* on plains of Xi'an.
"Expel"
Standing on the grassy plain, he reviewed his surroundings. Generally flat and with what appeared to be solid hard ground.

Looking around the large open field he confirmed that the few buffalo grazing here and there were its only inhabitants.

"Survey substructure" he instructed the *ATS*.

"Subterranean free of underground rivers" whispered the *ATS* in his mind.

"Subterranean structure mostly granite rock from volcanic activity...now dormant" continued the voice in his head.

The plains of Xi'an appear to be the perfect place to construct this step-pyramid.

"Now to find the local War Lord and then push him in the right direction!"

Power...greed, folklore, or fear, which temptation would be the way to motivate emperor Xiashian?

The only way to decide would be to enter the town and find out about how the locals live and more about their local folklore.

Entering the *ATS* he flies the still cloaked skimmer westward until he finds the town of Xianyang.

There he instructs the *ATS* to land,

"Expel"

Krys, still cloaked by his morph suit, now stood next to an old vacant barn. Wondering what garb to don, he notices a group of local villagers heading towards the gates of the town.

They were riding horses and wearing red robes. On their heads are small black round caps.

Deciding to blend in, he dons clothing of a similar nature and follows the group of men into the town.

In following the group of men, he observes various men and women with conical straw hats and blue worker jump suits, he sees the workers get to their knees and bow their heads as the red clad horse riders pass.

Within a few moments of the red clad horse group's passing, the workers got back up to their feet and resumed their previous business. This consisted mainly of haggling and selling their farm produce.

Seeing a tavern *Krys* breaks off from the group and heads straight for it knowing that he will get more of a flavour for the local customs after the patrons have had

105

a few tongue looseners. He presumed that the local brew in this tavern would be as potent as any other that he had visited.

Changing his outfit to that of a farm worker, *Krys* entered the dimly lit tavern.

Finding a seat close to a couple of intoxicated patrons, he sat down to listen.

"I heard that the great dragon of the North will come this winter and burn all the dead grasslands!" said the drunken patron closest to *Krys*.

"I know it happens every year and always at night, but this time I am going to stay awake and watch for him," slurred a particularly thin wrinkly man through rotting teeth.

The stench of his halitosis breath filled the air and is so strong even from across the table where he is sitting that *Krys* mentally instructs the suit to filter out the nauseating smell.

"We all know that the Lord Dragon flies in from his palace on the full moon when he means to show his displeasure," slurred halitosis man.

"We only see the results of what he did the night before though! I have never seen the Lord Dragon myself and don't want to!" spat the less drunk of the two.

"May the great emperor Xiahain protect us!" agreed halitosis man.

106

"I swear if it wasn't for him we would all be eaten by the Lord Dragon!" his slightly more inebriated brother in arms said, spraying the air with his words.

"A dragon?" thought *Krys*, *"Interesting!"*

This infatuation with dragons may be of some use to him.

Cloaking he left the tavern and entered the hot humid crowded street. Nearby *Krys* noticed a stable with an unattended horse poking its head out of the top half of the wooden stable door. Slowly so as to not startle the beast he made his way into the stable and stood besides the horse.

The horse snorted and started to shake, its nostrils flare with the smell of the intruder, muscles down it flanks ripple in agitation.

Krys projected a feeling of calm into the horse's mind.

The animal relaxed.

He de-cloaks and strokes the horse's mane. In response the horse *whinnies* and paws the ground.

Krys retrieves the stirrup and saddle from the stable wall and then fits them to the horse.

He re-engages the red robes, local looks and black hat.

Opening the stable door, he leads the horse out and into the street where he mounts the horse and heads further into the town.

107

"*Where did the men on horses go?*" *Krys* asked the *ATS.*

The image that is projected into his head shows a map of the town with a trail marked on it. The route shows a path with only a few twists and turns straight to the main courtyard of the current warlord, emperor Xiashian.

"*What are the red dressed horse riders doing now?*" *Krys* asked the *ATS* again.

"*They are unloading some leather bags.*" responded the *ATS*

"*It appears that some are filled with maps and survey equipment, others are filled with dried samples of the fauna and flora. From up here it seems like they must have collected these specimens on the journey they have recently completed.*

One bag has arm bands and daggers, all appear to be made of silver or gold." the voice whispered in his head.

Krys walks the horse up to the guarded gates of the courtyard.

Two men with pikes stand to attention and let him through. One of them makes a mumbled comment,

"*There's always one that gets lost! Probably strayed when travelling past the local tavern again!*" the guard coughed into his hand trying to make it seem as if he could not have voiced such a remark.

108

Krys followed the red robed men into the ornate Quora styled house. The gables were painted a bright blue and are carved into what appeared to be curled up dragon's tails at the end of each artichoke leaf style roof.

Krys looked up at the apex of the roof.

Dragon faced gargoyles peer down at him from each of the roof's corners. One snarling...One biting...One smiling and the last one breathing fire. They stand menacingly in their efforts to ward off any intruder.

Somehow, he will have to use this infatuation with dragons to his advantage.

The men in red are proceeding deep into the depths of the house; *Krys* follows them at a slightly slower pace trying not to be conspicuous. After a few minutes they enter a long hallway and prostrate themselves in front of a large jewel encrusted golden throne.

The pattern work on the chairs is mainly made up of miniature dragons. Some are flying; some spitting fire and others are tearing their victims apart caught in the act of swallowing the remnants of human extremities.

Following their example *Krys* prostrates himself, imitating the leader of the other red robed men. Their

109

small black hats were now removed and placed to the right of each humbled man.

A gong banged accompanied by the sound of flute music and blowing trumpets...then silence.

Krys, head down hears the swishing of silk on silk as the Emperor walks to his throne and sits.

"My loyal servants...raise your faces so I may see who it is that must be rewarded or for that matter punished," said the Emperor; his voice soft but somehow menacing.

Every prostrate man strained to hear what it is the Emperor was saying. They know that to disobey, even if they have not heard the command, would mean a painful death at the hands of the Emperor's royal guard.

All sit up, eyes downcast.

There seems to be a leader of the group and he looks up at the Emperor, then prostrates himself again.

"May I speak o great one, Lord of the Dragon and governor of all that his great eyes can see?" said the head of the red clad group.

"What is your name?"

"I am called Chinnea, oh great one."

"Then speak Chinnea, tell me of your trip to the North...Did you see a dragon?"

Chinnea proceeded to tell the emperor of the long and perilous trip that he and his companions had to endure on route to the northern lands.

There was many a time when bandits almost succeeded in cutting their throats and making off with the samples they had collected for the Emperor. On one occasion the bandits almost made off with the gold and silver they had traded their fine silken wares for.

Getting impatient, the emperor stood in a short sharp motion and shouted,

"BUT DID YOU SEE ANY DRAGONS?"

"No...no my lord, no dragons." whispered Chinnea, knowing that this could be his last day on Earth.

The Emperor slumped back down into his throne.

All of the red dressed men, including *Krys,* prostrated themselves again in front of the Emperor.

"How much gold and silver is there to be taken from these barbarians in the North?" demanded the Emperor.

Feeling the noose loosen slightly for the moment, Chinnea took a deep breath and then replied,

"My lord there is gold on every man, woman and child, it is as if they have as much of it as we have grains of rice."

"Do they have an army? Are they peaceful?

Can we trade with them or must the gold be taken by force?" the Emperor questioned, drool slipping from

111

the side of his mouth, the menace in his eyes betraying his *greedy* thoughts.

Feeling that the Emperor's infatuation with dragons; gold and power were his key to getting this pyramid built, *Krys* projected into Emperor Xiashian's mind

"Look to the sky tonight! A dragon of legend will come to visit you. The dragon rider has a great honour to bestow on you!"

The Emperors eyes cloud over for a moment, then with a manic grin, he shouts,

"Out,

OUT! ALL OF YOU OUT!

I must rest...for it has been foretold to me that a dragon will appear to me tonight!

GO...go now!"

With that, all of the red robed men including *Krys*, get up and genuflecting proceed backwards towards the door. They make sure that their backs never face the Emperor as this would be a sign of disrespect and result in an immediate loss of the offender's head.

Krys, once clear of the room, cloaked and then disappeared. The head of the red robes had been glancing quizzically at him, so it was time to vanish...literally. He would return tonight in a dragon ship and all the dragon rider attire he could get the *Morph-Suit* to conjure.

112

Heading back to the plains of Xi'an *Krys* went to do some research. He must make a grand impression tonight.

When the full moon was approaching its zenith, *Krys* entered the *ATS*. Mentally projecting an image of a Chinese dragon to the *ATS* the biomechanical entity shimmered and transformed itself.

A great black and green scaled serpent like monster took form out on the plains of Xi'an. The projected reek of sulphur hung heavily in the air.

"Project Fire Breath!" instructed *Krys*.

A plume of fire issued from the front of the *ATS*.

Krys looked at the dragon's fire breath unconvinced that it appeared authentic.

It must be perfect, a megalomaniac the Emperor may be, but he was no fool.

"Expel"

Standing on the grassy plain, *Krys* looked up at the projected image of the dragon.

The image was a little too folk-lorish, not quite what he had in mind. He then changed his mind on how to approach the appearance of the *ATS*.

Krys mentally projected a picture of a space ship covered in glistening black and green scales with the head and tail of a dragon to the *ATS*.

He stands back to admire his creation,

"Bigger teeth,

113

More Snarl...
Red Glowing Eyes...
Bristling Spiky Mane...
Talons for Landing Feet." instructed *Krys.*

The alien looking mechanical flying dragon turned to look at him, its menacing presence all too clear.

"Fire Breath" commanded *Krys.*

The *ATS* expelled a sulphurous smelling torrent of heat and fire directly at *Krys.*

"SHIELD!"

Krys's morph-suit reacted immediately, deflecting the flames harmlessly away.

The suit would have protected him, taking most of the damage had he not used the shield, but he would have required healing. He would have had to spend a few hours back in the embryonic sac of the *ATS* regenerating his burnt extremities and he did not have the time for that!

"Now to prepare the dragon-suit! Not too ornate though; more other worldly than dragon."

Besides he wanted to be in control of the space dragon, *not be a dragon*!

Krys projected an image of a dark oval reflective helmet, skin tight black and green snake like rubbery jump suit. The one-piece outfit shimmers as he moves,

114

like the scales of a snake! His feet are clad in dragon armour like talon boots.

Every time he moves there is a metallic clink.

"That will do!" thought *Krys* satisfied with his appearance.

Sitting on top of the dragon, *Krys* issues another command,

*"*Xiashian's *courtyard...Fly me there."*

The ATS performs its role perfectly in this theatrical deception as it rises into the air.

Vocalising a screech and breathing fire, it sets off for the town of Xianyang.

*

Back at Xiashian's court the Emperor paces nervously up and down.

"What if the dragon does not come?" the Emperor worried to himself.

The moon is about to reach its zenith and where is the dragon he knew would come.

"There will be dissension amongst my subjects, not that I'm too worried about that, but it's just such a waste of resources and gold, finding and cutting off all those disloyal heads," mused the Emperor.

"In any case it's probably about time to instil a bit of fear amongst them again. Fear is good for the masses; how else do you control them?

115

Maybe I should start a cult or combine all of their spirit gods into one all powerful god. Create a priesthood which I can control, now that's the thing to do!" soon he will give the instructions.

"Where is that *damn* dragon?" he mutters again to himself.

He hears a shout from one of his guards

"LOOK...LOOK UP IN THE SKY...THE DRAGON COMES!"

The guards as one fall to the floor of the courtyard covering their heads with as much hand and arm that can be humanly spared.

"AT LAST, MY DAY HAS ARRIVED!" shouted the Emperor.

The *ATS* twists and turns in the night air, a silhouette on the shining moon.

Flames roar from the front of the *ATS*, wings appear to flap and make a loud whoosh with every beat that they make.

Krys instructs the *ATS* to hover above the Emperor, the stench of sulphur fills the air.

The Emperor, finally in awe of those red evil eyes fixated on his, falls to his knees.

With outstretched arms, he shouts above the roar of the dragon's flapping wings,

"I implore you O Mighty Dragon of the Moon and Sky, what do you command? Tell me what you wish of me and it shall be so!"

"BUILD ME A GREAT STEP-PYRAMID. THE DETAILS WILL BE SENT TO YOU IN A DREAM," the dragon roared.

Krys projected an image of a pyramid similar to that of the one being built in Giza to the mind of the Emperor.

From above, the view below shows men and animals scurrying around like ants, using ropes and towers, to aid the stones being raised up the ramps and then levered into place.

Krys was disappointed. He quite liked his snake scale jump suit, but it looks like he will not need to use it as the modified *ATS* was more than up to the task,

"I will send a messenger with white hair and beard to aid you in your construction efforts. *Nothing must prevent the building of this great structure*!" continued *Krys* with the mind link.

The *ATS* beat its dragon wings harder and then rose into the air. Not a flaming torch is left burning as they are all extinguished from the powerful downdraft created during the *ATS's* assent.

The *ATS* screeches, bellows out more dragon breath and sails up and away into the night.

117

Krys and *ATS* are once again silhouetted against the back drop of the full moon.

The following morning *Krys* dons his usual grey gown and white-haired appearance. His white beard whisks in the morning breeze as he sets off westward towards the town of Xianyang.

Krys has an Emperor to *advise*!

*

INDIA

Chapter 10

250 BC:
Earth
India

Vejay was on his way to make an offering to the happy Buddha in the town square.

Although he was born of a lowly caste family, life has been better for him since King Asoka had converted to Buddhism. Tolerance towards him and his people has increased, and they had been generally accepted as human beings with the right to better their lives and that of their families and not merely survive on the handout of others. On the odd occasion he had even received a kindly word and some fresh fruit from some of the rural farmers.

It was just ten years ago that he was beaten and spat on every time he came to the town to make an offering. Now more and more people of all castes were converting to Buddhism.

Dressed in the blue sari of his caste everyone who sees him knows that he is from the lowest caste of their society and as such he kept his eyes downcast to avoid any unwanted attention.

Making his way towards the Buddha shrine, he notices a sacred cow kneeling in the street.

120

In the South of India all make an effort not to disturb the cow as it is a sacred beast and revered in this region of southern India. All are vegetarian, and any person caught consuming the flesh of the sacred beast would soon be stoned to death.

Apparently up North they partake of the flesh of this magnificent animal; he shudders at the imagery. Then to his horror, wonders what the flesh of the sacred cow would taste like and immediately chastises himself for having such impure thoughts. He slaps himself hard through the face to remind him that he is on his way to the Happy Buddha shrine and all his thoughts should be pure.

Whilst deep in thought of being pure and untainted Vejay almost forgot about the sacred cow in the road.

Whether by mistake, or someone wanted to put him in his place just as it was in the old days, he felt a slight push on his right shoulder. Off balance and a bit feeble from lack of food, he had only eaten naan bread with a few lentils yesterday morning; he fell heavily on top of the sacred reclining beast.

With a disgusted snort and a shake of the head the cow lumbered to its feet and started to back away.

Vejay immediately got down on his hands and knees and started to beg for forgiveness from the deity representative. Cursing himself for his stupidity he

121

carried on begging for forgiveness, then started to wail, vocalising his shame for all to see.

But it was too late, the damage has been done.

For all the new-found tolerance to his caste's sect with King Asoka's conversion to the peaceful ways of Gautama Buddha, he knows that his life is in great peril.

A crowd was gathering...

Someone cast a small rock...

It hits him full on the *temple...*

Stunned, bloodied and dazed he turned to where he thought the stone had been cast from, his eyes searching for *mercy.*

The next larger stone hits him square in the face shattering his nose, soon after he felt his jaw *shatter* with the impact of the next rock. *Then* something bigger hit him at the base of the skull. Vejay sank to the ground; soon all that was left for his wife to identify was a bloody pulp where once there had been the face of an emancipated human being whose only crime was the intent to worship at the feet of the Happy Buddha.

Compassion and tolerance for one's fellow neighbour seemed a long... long... way...away.

*

As trade with India's neighbours increased, Buddhism rapidly spread to Thailand, Sri Lanka and China.

122

FIRST CONTACT

Krys was pleased with the progression of Buddhism. The more people who converted to a single deity religion the better. It will make his task that much easier when the time came for him to unite the human race against the *Xhoseti*,

"Activating the weapon is one thing but getting mankind to think as one at the appropriate time would be an almost impossible task. Unity through religion may just be the key!" thought *Krys*, mentally adding this as an option for the impending doom that AD 2492 would bring.

Krys was certain that he or his genetic offspring could get the weapons built...that would not be the problem. The unity of mankind will and always will be the main issue as over the next few thousand years when the religious wars start there will be a tremendous number of vendettas to be resolved. Man, as always thrives on the pleasure of hurting those who had hurt them or their families. Forgiveness and reconciliation are still alien concepts to modern man, as civilized as they may think they are.

Who may be the outright winner, or even winners, will still need to be to be seen.

All *Krys* knows is that if there is one world dominating religion and one world dominating political governing body, mankind has a greater chance of survival against the *Xhoseti*.

123

When the *Xhoseti* arrive through the wormhole in AD 2492, man must be united.

United they stand, fractured they fall!

Krys in the cloaked *ATS* heads off to check on the progress of the three fail-safe pyramids being constructed by the *Guardians*.

If he knew anything about those strange Moa like looking *Guardians*, then he knew they would complete the pyramids on schedule. He and the rest of mankind were all counting on it.

"If there's one thing the Guardians are, it's efficient!" Krys mentally projected to the *ATS*.

"Where to next?"

Time and space seem as one, again that silky feeling...

*

ROBERT J STEPHENS

EARLY

ROME

FIRST CONTACT

Chapter Eleven

40 BC:
Earth
Rome

Krys had been observing the rise of this mighty empire for over the past six hundred years.

"Their thirst for conquest seems to show no bounds!

Bloodlust, rape, murder, plunder and the enslavement of any who oppose them appear to be the main drivers in the constant struggle between the squabbling ruling families. Should come in handy!

They would do anything it would appear to get a foot on the enemy's throat and then stamp...and stamp hard." *Krys* remarked to himself.

Alliances, oaths and blood bonds are made and broken on a daily basis. There was so much *vicious* infighting that *Krys* feared for his plans to unite the human race against the *Xhoseti*, although some aspects of their ruthless brutality would need to be cloned for future use.

Rome had carved with the sword an empire the likes of which mankind has not previously seen on Earth. It reminded him of one of the planets in Termites' galaxy that used a similar brutality to enslave their local populous but on a far grander scale.

Even if mankind could band together at the last hour against a single common enemy, it would be disorganised and too little...too late.

In the Roman society wives were divorced and remarried at the mere hint of a political advantage with another family or fortune, the feelings and emotions of the affected entities barely even considered.

Any who did not appreciate the ways of political deception were quite literally thrown to the dogs; that was of course after their throats had been cut or their bellies sliced open for the starving rabid mongrels to tear at and then fight over bloodied strips of human flesh.

Prodigy was bred, not under the auspiciousness of family love and respect, but to be bartered and traded as one would do with cattle in a market, all for a slight political advantage.

Conquering nations, creating civilisations, organising religions and pushing the human race towards one goal is all part of *Krys's* remit. So, the Roman Empire should really be a blessing in disguise, but *Krys* has his doubts.

Now that the pyramids in Egypt, China, Atlantis and Japan are complete, it was time to sow the seeds of organised religion and social cohesion.

The Atlantian and Japanese pyramids have been completed by the *Guardians* who had then submerged them to the bottom of their respective oceans.

*

The major singular deity religion of the era is that of the Hebrews of Judah.

The problem with Roman conquest is that, to avoid local rebellion, the newly conquered peoples could continue to follow and worship their own religious sects and deities. Rome, unlike other conquering megalomaniac nations, did not impose their own religious rules on the conquered. They simply incorporated the newly acquired gods of the conquered nation into their own very extensive list of deities and demigods. They appeared to have a god for every occasion. Jupiter was the king of gods, Juno the queen of gods, Mars the god of war, Venus the god of love, Apollo the god of the sun, Neptune the god of the sea, the list goes on and on...

This in itself is a problem, as praying to too many deities, had it been forced upon the conquered, would divide humanity and end up in their eventual destruction.

What was needed is a strong Roman Emperor who believed in one God over any other and would impose this belief on all his subjects and then enforce that single deity religion on all with an *Iron Fist and Will.*

With the demise of Julius Caesar there has been an internal conflict in Rome that should conclude over the next few years. Sides have been drawn, troops were being mustered, and an almighty battle will decide the fate of the Roman Empire and with it the religious fate of the known world. All *Krys* had to do was *watch* and *wait!* Should his intervention be required by the *Guardians* then he would assist, but until then he would stand by, intent on merely giving advice as he saw fit.

If Octavius was the victor, then *Krys* might be able to influence him on moral virtues and family values to unite the current civilized human population. The uncivilized world would have to wait until opportunity reared its head. The people of Rome have become obsessed with the immediate pleasures of the flesh. *Drunk* with power they debauch themselves at every opportunity.

However, if Marcus Antonius emerges the victor *Krys* would need a different tactic; the man revels in debauchery.

For *Krys*, becoming a member of the senate and having the ear of the wealthy and the influential will be of the utmost importance.

129

He will need to put plans in motion immediately after the battle has been concluded.

*

Krys landed the *ATS* on the westerly edge of the plains of Mars just outside the city of Rome. This was the traditional gathering place for the Roman Army during the month of March...the month for *War*. It is located to the North of Rome in order to show the barbarians of the interior the might of the Roman army. Each Roman general knew that there were always spies amongst the ranks of the conquered troop battalions and made sure to show the full strength of the Legions, so all might tremble and despair at ever trying to attack the Roman centre of the world.

Krys exited the *ATS* and de-cloaked, dressed in the Roman toga of a country businessman. he surveyed his current surroundings before moving on.

Stepping out from behind a large poplar tree he encountered a procession of purveyors of market goods heading for the northern gates of Rome, intent on getting them to the central square for sale.

Joining the group, *Krys* walked with them for a few miles to the gates and then past the guards and into Rome.

Krys needed to find out more about the local ways and customs of the current populous of Rome.

He had witnessed the amazing engineering feats that Roman engineers have achieved over past centuries and being suitably impressed knew that this was a critical time period for him and the *Guardians* to sow the seeds for their long-term plans. With an unlimited enslaved workforce there would be no limit as to what the Roman engineers could achieve as far as physical labour was required. Their only limitation would be their lack of technical knowledge or building materials.

When it came to long term planning though, one must think and plan ahead. To proceed without an organised design plan could be disastrous.

Structures built, or towns constructed would turn to dust in a matter of centuries as foundations collapsed or water tables changed due to over-construction and bad-planning. The city planners of Rome were plagued with this problem, which could be seen on a daily basis. The word *'Crisis'* would be quite apt.

In the older sectors of the city sink holes appear randomly and entire houses fall into the mines that run below the city.

The first miners who constructed the underground tunnels were just a memory of the past. With the cave-ins and lack of forethought no one now knows where the mining tunnels run, nor when they will swallow

131

another structure along with its inhabitants. Rome has been a victim of its own rapid success and expansion.

Due to the rapid population explosion, Rome now has approximately one million inhabitants and along with that growth many other unsavoury issues need to be addressed. With that large a population, the onset of disease, caused mainly by poor sanitation and a lack of clean drinking water, followed.

A system of water transportation and sewerage removal was desperately required. Roman engineers were constantly working on the aqueduct systems, some old and antiquated, some new and untried to bring fresh water to the masses.

Bathing was common practice, with the bath houses becoming gathering places for all citizens of Rome. Many an alliance has been made and broken in these houses of sanitation.

With the increase in population, other more earthly problems have reared their ugly heads. There are more mouths to feed and that means more waste to dispose of.

The Cloacae Maxima or sewerage disposal tunnels are constantly being upgraded and run under the city like a group of knotted tree roots.

If it had not been for this hidden gem under the city though, disease would soon have wiped out most of the inhabitants of Rome. When it came to technologically advanced building materials though, Rome has been especially fortunate.

Under the city runs an oxide rich volcanic rock deposit, created millions of years ago when the local volcanoes were still active. This rock deposit, when mixed with lime, aggregate and ash forms an incredibly strong and durable type of concrete. This form of concrete would even set and harden in seawater.

This lime volcanic ash mixture has ensured that Roman structures have stood the test of time and probably would continue to do so for many centuries still to come.

Concrete was the preferred material of construction for the Cloacae Maxima, as it sets even in the muddied water of the sewers; simply add sea water to the mix and leave to harden. A fantastical solution to the sewerage problem had been found by the ingenious Roman engineers.

Urine on the other hand was collected to be used for all manner of tanning and personal hygienic uses.

As *Krys* walked around the artisan areas of the city, the smell of the tanning vats mixed in with human sweat was almost over powering. Luckily, he could filter out the olfactory intrusion with his morph-suit. *Krys* found it strange that the people residing here did not seem to notice the awful smell; they appeared to be olfactory blind so to say.

133

Then again, it was amazing what the human brain could block out given time, or perhaps they were simply just used to it.

*

Whilst walking around the streets of Rome, *Krys* ventured into a particularly seedy part of the city's underbelly. The graffiti on the alley way's walls are particularly crude and extremely vulgar. Nothing had been left to the imagination. The artist had graphically depicted vulgar scenes of depravity. Further down the alleyway *Krys* noticed a tavern and started to make his way towards it. The sign above the tavern depicted a bull's decapitated head. Bright red blood dripped from the severed neck of the once magnificent beast.

Dressed in leather arm bands, brown cotton tunic and sporting a wide leather belt, the belt-buckle dull grey steel, *Krys* entered the reeking tavern.

Half naked women carouse with drunken patrons, that was, of course while the unwitting victim's coin lasted. A few men lie sprawled across table tops; face down, empty earthenware cups dribbling the last remnants of a dark red liquid.

Through the haze of the smoke ridden room a blond-haired young slave girl is going from one unconscious patron to another searching pocket and pouch. Most are empty already, their contents either

134

drunk or stolen. A pile of tangled human shapes lie heaped in every corner of the tavern, some stir, some appear to have been left to rot. The stench of faeces and urine was thick in the air. It leaves a foul taste in the mouth and can be smelt even above the stench of unwashed bodies, wine and stale ale.

In one dimly lit corner, there are a group of blue tunic clad men, holding down a young boy and taking turns raping him. The boy has a glazed look in his eyes; as if he has accepted his fate, knowing that this is his allotment in this hell hole. Life was just that, life...

Once the men have finished with him, they tossed a few coins at the boy and laughing turn and then leave the tavern. *Krys* follows them a few moments later.

They must be part of one of the Aventine gangs from the West quarter that he had heard so much about. They control all the Egyptian grain that was received down in the dockyards. Apparently, the grain was being used by Marcus Antonius to ensure leverage over the masses. If he controls the grain, he controls the bread and with it the mob.

If the Roman mob was on Marcus's side then he would have the power to rule Rome, even if only in an unofficial capacity.

Krys cloaks, but stands rooted to the spot, unsure of how he was going to deal with these ungodly, evil men.

The scene he has just witnessed stirs a *deep anger* inside him, his *blood boils*.

Life here is tough, so people do what they must just to survive. The wealthy and powerful pray on the weak and vulnerable, this is the way of the human being.

Krys must change this mentality.

With the disbanding of some of the army's legions due to a lack of war and enemies to fight, many of the discharged soldiers have no option but to join one of the many gangs in the poorer areas and get paid to do obscene tasks, some of rape and murder.

Any discharged soldier, even a battle-hardened war hero, would soon find himself lying dead in the gutter, a knife protruding from his back. All were fair game; even the women were to be feared here in this part of the Aventine's poorest quarter.

After a few too many jugs of wine, the drunken victim would most likely end up being robbed, beaten and eventually left in the gutter for the rats to feed on, unless they were sold into slavery. Just lying in the streets could kill a man, wounds would become infected and bacteria would do the rest, many a healthy man had succumbed to the smallest enemy on the planet.

Life was not only short and dangerous, but without funds, the filth in the streets would make short work of one's health.

136

To belong to a gang meant protection!

Each gang expressed their unity by wearing a particular coloured tunic or head band.

As *Krys* entered the alley to follow these evil men, he notices another group of men, dressed in the red tunics of another gang of the western Aventine area.

They draw their knives and set upon the blues in an instant. After a few scuffles, there are more reds than blues, the screaming and whimpering of the dying rapists fill the air. Within a few minutes all was quiet again.

A few dogs appear, lapping up the pools of blood and starting to *tear* hungrily at the corpses.

Krys moves on.

"Live by the sword, die by the sword!" flashes through his mind.

*

A few days later, dressed in his plain tavern tunic, sick of seeing the murder and rape of countless innocents, age and gender meaning little, *Krys* made his way eastwards. In fact, it would appear, the more *perverse* the crime the better for these *savages*.

Krys exited the murderous Aventine alleyways and then made his way towards the forum in the centre of the city. Soon he was standing in the Romanian, the city's central square. While he was waiting, a Roman

137

orator, carried by a troop of slaves, stopped in front of the Romanian lectern.

The slaves heave him to his feet; sweat glistening on their bulging muscles as they struggle with his great bulk. His position as the orator for powerful patrons has rewarded him handsomely and gluttonously as well. They ply him with all the food and drink that he could consume and consume it all he had! His nose and cheeks were a bright red; rings of wattle wobble around his extremities; every time he exhaled the fat around his neck shook with the excursion.

"Not much longer for this mortal plane!" thought *Krys.*

The orator produced a scroll, which he slowly unravelled. Taking a deep breath, waiting for the crowd to give him the attention he was hoping for, the obese man began,

"The once great and magnificent Marcus Antonius has been defeated and has now taken refuge in Egypt with his new wife Cleopatra, the Greek born queen of the Nile.

Gaius Octavius is now the new Emperor of the Roman Republic and will sponsor a feast of celebration for the next seven days."

The orator rolled up the scroll and with the help of his slaves was bundled back into his official litter. He was then slowly borne away by the six slaves who were carrying him.

"Now to get on the Senate," said *Krys* to himself.

*

Krys was walking towards the Senate building when a mob of approximately fifty *disbanded* soldiers and country *ruffians* storm the entrance to the Senate.

Krys can only envisage the following chaos and confusion that will follow should the Senate members be killed. He ran toward the Senate entrance,

"MORPH CENTURION," and with that he drew his sword and ran to protect the entrance.

The mob tries to get past him. He stabs the nearest man through the throat. Blood spurts from the gaping hole in his throat; the man falls to the floor clutching at the wound. His blood spills onto the marble floor making purchase almost impossible for the invading mob.

Krys's morph-suit has no such difficulty though, merely adapting his molecular friction requirements as soon as the slippery obstacle was detected.

Another ruffian tries to get into the Senate building; this one has a knife which he thrusts towards *Kry's* torso.

"MORPH SHIELD!" shouted *Krys.*
The blade struck his suit and broke in the man's hand.

139

The look of triumph in his brown eyes turned to shock as he stared into the piercing grey gaze of what must surely be a manifestation of Mars himself. *Krys* held the man's gaze with his own, then hit him square between the eyes with the pommel of his sword. The man went down in a heap of tangled arms and legs blood spouting from his smashed nose. A few more try to get past *Krys*, but the result is the same.

Soon there was a pile of bodies, some twitching, some convulsing and some deathly still lying in front of the Senate doors at *Krys's* feet.

Battle over; *Krys* hears a trembling voice behind him,

"*Soldier*, who are you?

Who sent you to save us?"

Thinking this is his opportunity to make an impression and get closer to the new Emperor; *Krys* stood to attention, fist to chest and gives a rigid straight arm salute.

"*Krys* Reenberg of the disbanded sixteenth...*SIR*. I have come to seek an audience with the emperor Gaius Octavius.

If he accepts me back into his army then it will have been the Emperor who has saved you!" shouted *Krys*.

FIRST CONTACT

"It will be our honour to introduce you to the
Emperor, with I might add, my own personal
recommendation as a reward for such bravery."

*

A few days later *Krys* was summoned to Octavius's
Palacium situated in the wealthy northern sector of
Rome.

"Come, sit next to me centurion. Ciscerian here has
been telling me of your heroic deeds in front of the
Senate. Saving, it would appear single handily, all of
their not too frail gluteus maximums on which they rely
so heavily," said Octavius to *Krys*, a mocking chuckle in
his voice.

"But enough of the small talk!

I have no record of you being in the sixteenth, even
though it was disbanded last year. I will of course
revive it when it is needed again, and you are more
than welcome to join up then," Octavius paused to
study this hero.

"So...who are you, not a Gaul spy or assassin?

I daresay from the reports of your prowess with a
sword, all of Rome is at your mercy."

Krys thinking on his feet, as this could turn out very
badly for him and his plans for the emperor, replied
smoothly,

"*My Emperor*, I am no Gaul, but I do represent a council of the highest authority.

I am here to spread the message of piety and family values," *Krys* paused and looked the Emperor straight in the eyes, holding his gaze, before continuing,

"If the Roman people continue with the debauchery and blood thirst that is upon them now, then there will be famine and plague. The rodents will run wild in the streets; babies will be born defective and deformed.

I implore you end the evil ways of the men of Rome!"

Octavius, staring straight back into *Krys's* grey eyes,

"Stranger, this is a problem that has been plaguing my dreams for many a Lunar cycle. It would appear that you have come at an opportune moment. This must be a sign from the gods...And with the Senate and you to back my reforms the people of Rome will gladly embrace and enforce these new acts of piety."

"Thank you Emperor. You may not realise it, but you have done *mankind* a great *service*.

As to my presence here in your villa, tell the senate that I am a guest of your household and then send me away to the provinces, so I may spread your new laws." said *Krys* solemnly to the Emperor.

"*I must leave now though!*" *Krys* then projected into the mind of Octavius.

142

FIRST CONTACT

"Are you sure that you won't stay for the orgy later? I hear that the Slavic female slaves are all virgins and the wine is made from crushed grape husks that were squeezed between their naked toes. Something named brandy-wine I am led to believe. Apparently, it makes the girls really open to suggestion and by that, I mean really open to new ideas and experimentation." said Octavius.

A look of disappointment spread across *Kry's* face. This was going to be harder than he thought.

"No...I will not be joining you in your orgy of depravity and you should slow down with all these young girls as they will put a strain on your essence. You will need your strength for the upcoming conflict with the Senate and you cannot afford to fail...The fate of mankind depends on it!" projected *Krys*.

With that *Krys* stood up and walked toward the room's exit, then after a few steps into the adjoining corridor cloaked and vanished.

After speaking about family bonds and values, *Krys* suddenly felt all alone, and for the first time since he was woken from stasis feels isolated from the very species that he is trying to save. He has a deep yearning for a friend, maybe even a partner and companion.

Krys entered the *ATS* and not knowing or even caring where his next assignments were started to sink

143

into the all-embracing grasp of the biomechanical entities embryonic regeneration sac.

"*Where to?*" whispered the *ATS* in his mind.

"I'm done not knowing and I do not even care...ask the *Guardians*," replied Krys via the mind link.

After a few moments the cloaked *ATS* rose into the air and set a path for Ireland.

Somehow *Krys* knew where they were traveling to but did not understand why he was drawn to that particular part of the world, only feeling a pull in the back of his mind that something important was about to transpire.

Time and space seemed as one...

That silky feeling again...

Soon the green and pleasant landscape of *Killarney, Ireland* filled his mind.

*

FIRST CONTACT

IRELAND

145

Chapter Twelve

10 BC:
Earth
Ireland

It was while on a routine progress check-up flight over Britain, West over the Druidic island of Anglesey, he felt the need, no... more of a push inside his head, to land in a village in the south of Ireland, a place called Killarney; it was there that he met *her*.

He had taken on the guise of a local villager, enquiring here and there as to the state of the king's health and when his daughter was to marry. He was asking questions of the local blacksmith when he was hit over the head with something heavy. His morph suit took most of the impact, stunned; he fell to the ground.

Instead of getting up and teaching these ill-mannered ruffians a lesson, he lay there and listened to them discussing his fate.

"The king wants him alive and unhurt!" stated one of the attackers.

"There are strange tales of a grey cloaked old man who appears from the East, and when he vanishes, life as we know it changes forever, not always for the better I might add. *Time to play the questions and answers game with our stranger! Get our guest and put him in the stockade."*

Krys was bundled up and carried to the main building in the centre of the village.

The largest building in the village was a stone built round building some two storeys high with a thatched roof and large thick oak doors. Inside *Krys* was carried down some stairs to a small dimly lit cell with iron bars and a weight-based locking mechanism of a sophisticated and what appeared complex nature; the blacksmith in this village must be a man of extraordinary talent!

On the floor is a small wooden three-legged stool and some sparsely scattered damp straw, but not much else. The 'dopp......dopp' dripping sound of water droplets hitting a bowl of water was the main source of disturbance...along with the occasional squeak and scuffle of some small rodents sparring over the scraps of uneaten food that had been discarded or left to rot by the previous unfortunate tenants.

Dropping *Krys* unceremoniously on the floor, the group of thugs left and returned the way they entered; one of them locked the iron gates with a large but many faceted iron key.

Krys slowly...feigning injury in case someone was watching, got to his feet, pulled the stool towards

147

himself and sat down to await his tormentor's pleasure.

Escape would be easy enough, but he was intrigued and willing to bide his time until he could confront his attackers' master.

A few hours later the king and a few of his henchmen arrive at his cell. All have swords and are wearing a combination of leather with strips of steel banded in a cross pattern through their armour. The king, having been offered a stool, sits down in front of *Krys,* staring at him through the gaol's bars.

Clearing his throat, the king broke the silence,

"We hear tales of a grey cloaked Druid that wanders here and there all over the British Isles seeking to spread word of change and creating a great fuss with it...

All who are touched by this grey cloaked devil are bewitched! Are you that grey cloaked devil?" the king stared at *Krys* with piercing grey eyes, a flock of curly white hair crowns his head, his beard is as white as *Krys's*, they look so alike they could be brothers.

The king coughed; a rattling sound reverberating in his chest as he took a slow deep breath interjected by restrained, controlled bouts of shallow coughing.

"Your majesty, I am the grey cloaked man you seek; however, I am not the devil seeking to upset the way that you govern your lands...

148

FIRST CONTACT

I am however interested in how many priests you have and to what deity do you and your kin bend your knee?" *Krys* ended the reply with a question of his own.

The king coughed again and waits, his face bulges a deep crimson purple reddish colour with the effort of controlling the coughing outburst. Then unable to contain the instinctive need to expel the phlegm from his lungs, he bursts into an uncontrollable bout of painful rasping coughs...blood flecked his lips.

The chest rattle, like a rasp being drawn over dried wooden planks, sounded painful with each breath the king took.

Krys stood and then raising his hand, projects a humming, oscillating sound towards the king's chest, shaking the blocked bronchial vessels in his lungs until they released their stale and poisonous sputum into his oesophagus. With a huge choking upheaval, the king vomited this vile, bloody and mucus filled ball of poison onto the floor and lay quivering on the cold stone floor.

In alarm, the king's guards draw their swords and attempt to get inside the cell to stop *Krys* from continuing the *witchcraft* he was performing on the king. All they know is that the grey cloaked man in the cell is attacking their king with some kind of *evilness* and must be stopped.

In the confusion and uncoordinated scramble to release the complicated locking mechanism, they were

149

taking too long to reach *Krys*; one of the guards pulled a knife from his scabbard and threw it at *Krys*.

"Shield" commanded *Krys* calmly.

The man's knife deflected harmlessly off his morph-suit and dropped to the ground where it clattered on the stone floor of the dungeon.

Krys, finished with the healing process, lowered his hand and sat back down onto the stool.

"*STAND DOWN!*" shouted the king.

Standing to his feet the king took a shallow breath, no rattle evident, and then the king drew in a huge draft of fresh air. Still no rattle evident!

The guards stopped trying to get into the cell and turned to stare at the king now standing before them. He appeared taller; the stoop all but eliminated from his previously pain racked frame.

Standing before them is the king of old before he took ill, strong and proud, a glint of steel in his grey eyes.

They all kneel as one, including *Krys*.

"*GET THE STRANGER OUT OF THERE!*

A FEAST...PREPARE A FEAST!" boomed the king.

The guard with the gaol key unlocked the prison gate and let *Krys* out.

"*Krys* come on...Catch me if you can!"

The king turned and rushed out of the room, taking the stairs two at a time. A howl of laughter tracking his

150

progress up the stairwell as the healed king bolted up the stairs taking them two at a time.

*

Later that evening twenty-one curved half moon oaken tables are placed in a circle in the centre of the village. Wild boar, deer and a heifer are roasting over wood burning fires, the flames low so as to not burn the freshly slaughtered animals. The smell of fat dripping down onto the glowing embers makes for a mouth-watering experience. As the fat drips down the flanks of the succulent spiced flesh and makes contact with the embers below, it makes a sizzling noise and lets off a puff of flavoured smoke which only serves to heighten the sensation. The mere act of a feast bonds the tribe together.

Even for a prosperous and organised village such as this, a full season's meat for the entire village was being cooked on this very night.

Later, the king stands at the head table to address the assembled villages,

"My fellow Killarney brothers and sisters, it is for our new-found Druidic friend, *Krys;* as he is known," the king gestured toward *Krys* sitting at one of the crescent shaped tables, "who comes to us from the East, that we will hold the first toast of health this evening.

151

I have found health and vigour thanks to his wise teachings and blessings," he winks at *Krys* in an all-knowing way.

"Krys...To your health!"

Each of the table's patrons stood and as one drained the first of the smooth sided wooden cups filled with beer placed in front of them. Once complete they all sit down awaiting the next toast.

"The next toast is as always is to my beautiful daughter Storm; let us give the second toast of health to her!

May she find a mate who is worthy of her and bear him many sons or daughters. All will be most welcomed at our hearth.

Storm! To your health!"

Again, the table's occupants rose and drained their second now fermented berry wine filled cups. All sit back down again to await the third toast.

"The third toast is to our ancestors...May they rest in peace, give us wisdom...patience...and guide us in times of need!

To the ancestors, for their wisdom and protection!"

This time the wooden cups were filled with the brown, fiery, molten barley fermented liquid from the north-men.

The water of life they call it.

Only the king has spoken during the toasting process; a silence of anticipation fills the air as mouths filled with saliva at the prospect of gorging on the bounty of smoked meat being prepared on the fires.

"AND NOW TO FEAST!

BARD...LET THE MUSIC BEGIN!"

Krys turned to the now slightly flushed king's daughter who had been seated beside him and marvelled at her eyes.

Grey like his! Her hair too, shock white just like his!

"How can this be?" mused *Krys*.

Somehow the *Guardians* have been playing genetic matchmaker or at least genetic deities.

"That would explain why the king's appearance is so similar to mine..." thought *Krys*.

A *Guardian's* voice in his head whispers,

"Krys, your time on Earth will be soon come to an end.

In the few years that you have left, you must sire an off-spring. His name is to be Chris Stormberg.

You will take him on the eve of his fourth terrestrial birthday to the ATS to transfer your knowledge and experience to him.

This young female has been genetically enhanced to be compatible with your altered DNA.

The rest is up to you. Remember the fate of mankind rests with you and your genetic offspring.

153

FIRST CONTACT

Do not fail!" warned the *Guardian's* voice in his mind.

Krys turned to look at Storm and she in turn changed her position to look back at him having almost felt his gaze upon her. She gave an involuntary shudder of pleasure,

"I feel like I have met you before. There is something very familiar about you," Storm shouted, barely audible over the music and cheering of the celebrating villagers.

The king was dancing with a few young maidens, probably intent on testing his new-found vigour later that evening.

Storm hears a voice whisper in her head,

"Give me your hand Storm," she passes her hand to *Krys*.

A tingling sensation passes between them. A slight buzzing sound emanates from the tiny minute blue sparks that flitter between them.

"Is that you in my mind Krys? Only papa and I can mind link like this!

It is strange how, now you are here, I can only sense you, I cannot sense papa anymore!"

They remain in thought contact throughout the night. *Krys* explained where he was from and what his mission was about. Not that anyone would believe her if she told anyone his tale, but he still gets her to swear

154

to keep his mission a secret. Storm does so with the mind link making the bond between them even stronger.

Storm then proceeds to tell *Krys* of what has come to pass in her village, how she and father were visited one night by strange lights and taken away to the stars by these strange beings in mechanical large headed suits.

They both came back changed, Storm for the better, papa not so much though. Since that visitation, she had not had any form of sickness or disease, papa though; he became very ill soon after, but never seemed to quite get better or sicker.

"Is that when you got the white hair, was it during the visitation?" questioned *Krys* with the mind link.

"Oh no!" blurted out Storm, "We have always had grey eyes and white hair; it has been in the family for as long as anyone can remember. It is written in our lore that only a white-haired king can take the throne of Killarney."

Eventually they fall asleep locked in each other's embrace, a bond of extraordinary strength and mutual respect had formed between the two genetically paired human beings. A bond born not of the stars as the *Guardians* had tried to initiate, but one of deep and mutual love for the other.

XHOSETJ

Just before dawn at the reddening of the sky, *Krys* stirs, Storm too awakens. They make love right there on the ground. They both feel the bonding of new life stir within her.

"I must return to my duties, but will come back as often as I can," projected *Krys* to Storm's mind.

"Remember there is always someone watching over you. It may be me; it may be one of the *Guardians, but you will always be protected!* If you are in any danger or in need of me in any way just think of me and I will be there as soon as possible." said *Krys* to Storm holding her face in his hands.

Nine months later a white haired, grey eyed baby was born in the village of Killarney.

Krys tried to return as often as possible, but with events unfolding as they were, time to spare was in short supply.

Rome was destroying his careful if somewhat hopeful plans one battle at a time, regress not progress seemed to be the theme of the day.

*

It is the year six BC.
It is time...

Four years later, as per the *Guardians* request, little *Chris* is about to undergo his transformation to manhood, *Guardian* style!

156

FJRST CONTACT

Chris has had such a short childhood, but the fate of mankind rests on this tiny and presently insignificant child. As per instruction, *Krys* and Storm take him to the *ATS*.

Krys returned to Killarney, walking in from the East as was his custom. Storm was waiting with young *Chris*, already mind linked with *Krys* and greeted him with a hug and a long deep kiss.

Chris, still a bit wary of this man in the grey robe who calls himself his father hangs back reservedly.

His father touches him on the shoulder and a spark crackles between them. *Chris* feels a stir deep within himself, then a voice whispers in his head,

"Chris, this is your father, we are linked together in a mind link with your mother. Please will you say something to your mother?"

"Mother!

Father! This is wonderful!

I feel you inside my head; it is like we are one! Father, I feel like I have always known you, that you are me!" exclaimed little *Chris*.

"Chris my son, I must take you with me on a short but vital journey. My time here on Earth is nearly spent and we do not have much time left together!

I must give you my knowledge from the past so that you will be able to complete our family mission."

157

XHOSETI

Kneeling in front of the young child, *Krys* softly whispers to his son, "Son...please... Come with me. It is time for you to meet your destiny.

I will introduce you to your best friend, it will keep you alive over your long and extended lifetime. It will nourish and protect you; it will be your chariot to the *Guardians*. There is nothing the *ATS* will not do for you; you will only need to ask of it. *Come*...time is rapidly running out for me, we must go...say goodbye to your mother."

Chris hugs his mother's legs, she bends down and picks him up, holding him tightly and kisses his face repeatedly, and then she hands *Chris* to *Krys*.

"See you shortly my dear," whispers *Krys* for her mind only.
Hand in hand *Krys* and *Chris* walk out of the village and head toward the cloaked *ATS*.

"Stand in front of the ATS Chris." projected *Krys* to the child's mind.

Both Krys and *Chris* can see the shimmering tube shape of the *All Terrain Skimmer* which would be invisible to any passing traveller.

"Place your hands on the skimmer." instructed *Krys*.

"Welcome Chris Stormberg," whispered the *ATS* in his mind.

"Please wait, verifying DNA

FIRST CONTACT

DNA verified
Entry?"
Chris under *Krys's* instruction replies with the affirmative.

A large proboscis like tube extends from the *ATS* and swallows *Chris* taking him deep into the belly of the biomechanical entity...

Krys turns away from the *ATS* and starts back towards the village to spend his last few mortal weeks on Earth with his beloved Storm. He hopes they will be re-united when all of this is done. That is presuming that *Chris* will be successful in uniting mankind and defeating the *Xhoseti*.

*

Chris, now inside the embryonic sac of the *ATS* awoke; terrified he started to thrash out screaming for his mother, he is after all just a four-year-old boy.

The *ATS* slowly...gently embraces *Chris* in the warm embryonic fluid, quelling his wild thrashing movements; slowly the child starts to relax and breathe in the rich oxygenated fluid. A long snake like tube attaches itself to his temple and calmness envelops *Chris* sending him to sleep.

The *ATS* had just issued a sedative via the connection; the procedure that was about to follow would be too painful for any human to consciously withstand and the mental scarring of the experience would damage *Chris* forever should he be conscious.

In addition to the *DNA* modifications that are to be bonded with *Chris's* genetic code for him to remain disease free during his long and extended levity, it is the rapid growth and ageing process to full adulthood that he must undergo for the enhancement to remain permanent.

Bones and muscles will have to broken and remade bigger and stronger over the space of just a few weeks. *Chris* was rendered unconscious, blissfully unaware of what is mechanically happening to his body and mind.

The tearing of flesh and breaking of bones started...
*

Three weeks pass and *Chris* stirs inside the *ATS*, he feels different...

Looking down at his naked body he marvelled to see the body of a fully developed male of twenty-five years of age slowly come into focus.

"Chris this will be unpleasant for just a few moments until the drugs take effect," whispered the *ATS*.

FJRST CONTACT

Images start to flash through his now fully developed mind, starting slowly then increasing in speed and volume.

The past *thirty-one thousand years* of *Krys's* memories flood into *Chris's* mind. A feeling of euphoria rushes through his body and mind, *"Aahh... thank goodness for chemicals!"* exclaimed *Chris* to the *ATS*.

Chris, almost devoid of physical sensation, now felt a far away pinching, pressing and clasping sensation running over the entirety of his body as the *ATS* massaged his newly formed body, stretching...testing and bulging newly formed muscles that need exercising. Probes and electric stimulation aid with the muscle toning procedure.

"Attaching morph-suit," the voice whispered in his mind.

An hour passes...

"Process complete!" exclaimed the *ATS* proudly.

Chris just wanted to get out of the *ATS* so he could test out his new body,

"EXPEL"

A moment later *Chris* was standing next to the *ATS* which was still cloaked. The sun is just rising, a red dawn cloaked the sky, bright streaks of yellow just starting to pierce the bloody veil.

161

FIRST CONTACT

"A new dawn for a new man!" he croaked to himself, new vocal cords being used for the first time.

Looking down at his naked body, he issues the command,

"Attire!"

A grey cloak forms and covers his body, a white beard forms on his jaw and cheek bones, his hair turns the same shade of white as his fathers. His hair and beard whisk in the cool morning breeze flittering with the slight gusts of wind that bathe his new body. The sensation of the wind touching and teasing his exposed skin gives him a gratifying feeling of belonging...it was as if Mother Nature was welcoming her newly born child into the world.

Taking a deep long breath of fresh air, he notices that the air is sweet but with a faint hint of smouldering fire.

Chris starts off towards the village, a little unsteady at first and then with growing confidence strides towards his intended destination picking up speed as he went.

When he arrived, the village appears to be dead, lifeless apart from a smoldering fire in the centre of the village. No one stirred, not even a dog comes skulking out of the shadows to welcome this new addition to the planet.

He mentally probed for his father and mother. His mother projects an image of where they are to his mind. Following her instruction, he finds the mud and straw-built cottage that *Krys* and Storm are in and enters through a straw mat door.

Krys was dying; lying on the hard-packed mud floor of the cottage, he looked over two hundred years old. His skin was cracked and looked like it is about to tear through to his frail and emancipated skeleton. His eyes bulge like that of a starving infant, but there is still a spark of life in them – *barely!*

Storm too is looking old; she must have been sharing energy with *Krys* to keep him alive for this very meeting with his newly formed prodigy.

"It is good...to see you my son...you are a fine young man...strong and able...the *ATS* has done a remarkable job. That white haired old man exterior doesn't fool your old mom though...I am sorry we could not spend...more time together...but time has finally caught up with me...and with your father." said Storm to her son lovingly, her voice cracking slightly when she spoke.

Krys using the last of his mental energy, projects to them both,

"I will need both of you to help me get to the ATS. There is still information that I can impart to you via the ATS.

163

Please...*Help me up.*"

Chris and Storm together pick up *Krys*, now weighing less than an infant. He is a mere husk of the former proud servant to the *Guardians*.

They carry him eastward to the *ATS* and stand him, hands touching the *ATS's* shell. A long tube extends to encase him and then just before he was about to leave, he turned to Storm,

"Goodbye my love and good luck my son." then the *ATS* swallowed him.

"Take me with you!" pleaded Storm, tears welling in her eyes.

Inside the embryonic sac *Krys* feels his mind starting to fade. The *ATS* starts to extract all the remaining memories not already imparted to *Chris*.

Krys takes his last liquid filled breath and with a throaty chest rattle the *Guardian's* servant ceases to exist.

The physical remains of *Krys'* body start to dissolve as the *ATS* absorbs any remnants of what was once the old grey cloaked human being *Krys...Nothing would be left to waste.*

Storm leaned against the shell of the *ATS* and mentally projects to the biomechanical entity,

"Take me as well! I have information that may help Chris and without Krys I do not want to remain here alone."

164

There was a long pause as if the *ATS* was in communication with someone or something.

"YOU MAY TAKE HER...

IT IS PART OF THE CIRCLE...

THERE MUST BE BALANCE," was the response from the *Grand Architect*.

With permission received, the proboscis like tube extended and swallowed Storm. Soon she has had her memories drained and stored in the *ATS*. Once complete the process of absorbing her physical body started and within hours she too was no more.

Suddenly, *Chris* felt very alone...then in his mind, an image of his parents appeared, and *Chris* knew they would always be with him; a part of them will live on in the *ATS* and in his mind forever.

One of these days he knows that he will join them *wherever they are.*

*

FIRST CONTACT

PALESTINE

Chapter Thirteen

1 BC
Earth
Palestine

The heat was unbearable! His water gourd was nearly empty – he must save what is left of the water for his heavily pregnant wife. They will need to rest soon though; she gets weaker and weaker as she nears term.

At least he was able to get a small cart and fill it with straw to give her some padding against the infernal jolting the wheels make every time that blasted donkey rode a stone.

The more he beat the cart pulling donkey for taking the bumpy route, the more the beast seems to take pleasure in going over the biggest of the road's stones. He had stopped whipping the donkey two miles back and the groans coming from Mary as the cart bumped along the path seem to have lessened.

"Maybe the donkey has sympathy pains for Mary and understands what she is going through - something mothers understand everywhere, even Romans and donkeys," thought Joseph.

Joseph raised his head to look at the landscape that had occupied his vision the past few days and cursed

167

the Romans again for making him and Mary go through this hellish trip.

Walking through the dusty shrub filled landscape, the small party of untagged men and women trudged along a path already travelled by thousands on their way to be registered in the new Roman census.

It takes two days to walk the ten miles westward from Nazareth to the city of Bethlehem in Galilee, but with a pregnant wife it will take a few days more!

They need to rest more often than the other travellers. She doesn't complain, but he knows she is uncomfortable and in pain.

He fears they won't make it to Bethlehem before she will be forced to give birth.

"She must be holding the baby in by sheer force of will. Who knows when that will not be enough?" he thought.

As they walk his mind wanders back to past events.

It has always been difficult for the chosen people, but the Roman task masters, always inventive, have just instilled a new way to inflict pain and suffering on them.

A few years ago, the Romans found a pocket of Jewish resistance fighters in the town of Sepphoris, just four miles to the northwest of Nazareth, so in typical Roman style proceeded to raze the entire town to the ground killing almost everyone there.

FJRST CONTACT

Resistance it would appear, is futile!

While he was trudging along the dusty path, his mind pleasantly went back to the night he was introduced to Mary.

Her father, Jacob, who owned one of the many workshops, had provided the feast and wine. The fires burnt high and there was much singing and dancing, but he only had eyes for Mary, so young and so pretty.

Her skin so soft and velvety to the touch...

A shiver of pleasure ran down his spine when he thought of that first encounter. Luckily it was before the Romans had tightened the noose that now enslaved them all.

From the ashes of Sepphoris a new hope had risen though. Now a new city named Tsipori was being built on top of the old town's remains. When it is completed, the city will be the most modern and well-planned city in all of Judea. He has seen the plans. They even have numbered streets, underground tunnels for removing excrement and even overland water carrying viaducts, aqueducts essentially.

"It is going to be *beautiful!*" said Joseph to the dusty road.

He has so much work ahead of him and with the prospect of work comes the hope of a better future. As head carpenter of Nazareth, he had been approached by some of the builders to start a carpenter's guild.

169

FIRST CONTACT

Like everything though, there was always a price to pay!

This time one of the conditions is that he and Mary must travel to Bethlehem to be registered for the Roman census. Something to do with a head count in the Promised Land!

He knows it's more about money than anything else!

Once counted, like the shepherd counts his sheep, they will know how much greater their empire is and how many subjects they can command taxes from. It can only be bad news for the likes of him and his kind.

It has been over sixty years since the Romans under Pompey the Great's strong arm came with sword and fire to take Bethlehem. His Father was young then. Still, the presence of those red clad soldiers was a constant reminder of just who *rules the Promised Land!* At least they did not try to stop the people of Judea worshiping in the synagogue. If they had, there would have been an immediate uprising. That was something the people would never stand for and the Romans knew it!

All who were willing to accept the yoke of the old king and then to simply change one master for another, in this case that of a Roman emperor, would have quickly changed their minds!

170

Instead the Romans embraced the Torah, very clever that! No wonder their empire was so vast.

The new emperor Augusta, the sly dog, had even put that Roman feet kissing traitor Herod on the Jewish throne. *Just to keep the peace!*

Pockets of resistance were starting to form though and are becoming more organised in their rebellion against the Romans every day. He had heard of groups of the more fanatical Roman Jews attempting to assassinate Emperor Augusta back in the great city of Rome.

It was probably Herod who ordered the counting of his flock; sure, he claimed he was ordered to do so by Augusta, but then why aren't the Jews in Rome being counted in the same way?

Something just does not add up!

"*How* can Herod expect pregnant women to make the long journey just so they can be tagged and counted? *And for what?*"

Joseph ground his teeth in frustration at the thought of the unfairness of this life.

"*Damn that megalomaniac!*"

He must remain calm though, he doesn't want to upset Mary, she has just got to sleep poor thing, and she was always so exhausted!

171

FIRST CONTACT

How long until she gives birth to the child? Surely only a day or two? She can hardly walk, never mind travel!

There is always some good news though.

The evenings are warm, stars shine brightly in the clear sky, no bandits have tried to rob them and it's just about time to stop and make camp for the evening.

As soon as they stop, Joseph set about making a small fire to warm the leavened bread they have brought with them.

They also have olives, cheese and a few strips of dried fish. He sets about getting their meal ready.

After supper, he pulled out a small gourd of diluted wine. Mary will only take water, but Joseph took a long deep draught from the wine gourd trying to clear the dust from his throat. His throat feels raspy and parched.

"Oh, to have this ridiculous registration over and to be back in Nazareth!" exclaimed Joseph.

The coolness of their home, the smell of the olive tree in the small courtyard, how in the morning the dew activated the smell of Corsican mint as his bare feet walked on them. He can still remember the sweet *minty* fresh smells early in the morning. That deep breath of the fresh crisp air clearing his head as it brought a smile to his face when he remembered the night before.

FIRST CONTACT

"Time to stop longing for something better and get some sleep!"

Tomorrow should be the last day on this dusty road. He went to check on Mary, she was sleeping soundly, a faint smile on her lips; the baby must be sending her pleasant dreams as they both slept. She let out a contented sigh. Joseph left her to her blissful slumber and returned to the fire. Pulling out the wine gourd he settled down for the evening.

*

In the morning, with the sun starting to peak over the dust laden red horizon, Joseph buried the now heat depleted ashes of last night's fire a few metres away from the road where they had camped.

After feeding and watering the donkey, Joseph hooked the beast up to the cart and started again on their journey westwards towards Bethlehem.

Mary stirred as the cart started to move slowly forward, but then rolled on to her side and went back to sleep. After an hour's slow progress...she woke,

"Husband, I just had the most wonderful dream!
We were all sitting in a barn...baby Jesus, that is what I shall name him, is wrapped up in a manger as we have no crib where we are going. Then three men enter the barn bearing gifts and kneel in front of baby

Jesus. They proclaimed Him to be the son of God!" explained Mary.

"I hope that we find that barn pretty soon as I think it will not be long now before our son arrives."

Smiling at her, Joseph takes Mary's hand in his and kisses it softly. How he loved her. He would move Heaven and Earth for her, anything she wanted he would give her no matter the cost to himself.

They travel on for another six hours; a few travellers pass them by, friendly sorts, generally smiling and waving. Shouting their good wishes for the new child that must surely soon arrive.

*

Chris was hovering in the *ATS* cloaked above Masada, an ancient Jewish fortress out in the Jordanian desert.

The fortress sat on top of a mountain and only has two access paths, one a snaking path on the East, the other a steep cliff face on the West. It has been used countless times as a retreat by various leaders of the Jewish people. It was even used as a refuge during some of the civil wars that had plagued the Jewish nation during its tormented history.

King Herod had made the fortress into a luxury retreat so that if he had need of it he would not have to be besieged in squalor. The ingenious water cisterns

174

are fed by the dam on the West side of the mountain via aqueducts and canals. These in turn were used to supply water to the Roman villa like rooms and baths that Herod had constructed.

Chris was just marvelling at the water storage and supply system when he received the summons to attend a meeting with the Guardians.

He instructed the ATS to take him to the Guardian Station in Earth's orbit. After docking with the station, he issues the command,

"Expel"

An image of the route he must follow into the station appeared in his mind and soon he was standing in a large empty room, lit by soft yellow glowing crystals on the floor and in the ceiling. Patiently Chris waited.

As far as first impressions go, this room had quite literally nothing to make it memorable. There are no features at all; it was simply a round softly lit room, no chairs or tables, no screens...nothing.

There was a faint humming noise and then a portion of the blank bare wall parted.

Six black clad vaguely humanoid figures with large heads and square features entered the room.

Expecting some introductions, Chris waited for them to begin. His father's voice whispered in his head to be patient, he feels his mother's hand rest on his

175

shoulder to calm him. That too was a first; it is very comforting and quite welcome though.

These black clad figures were a bit ominous though, luckily not menacing; the large heads seem perilously balanced on top of the tubular like humanoid bodies.

A voice inside his head spoke,

"Chris Stormburg, we the Guardians welcome you.

We have reviewed your human physiology and genetic structure and are pleased with the result. You are the reincarnated image of your father, both internally and externally," approval evident in the speaker's words.

"An event will unfold in the next few hours that is of great importance and will have a huge impact on the future of humanity."

Chris kept quiet and waited for this all-important event to be revealed to him.

"There is a baby boy that will be born in a stable close to the city of Bethlehem. We have projected the need for certain individuals to travel from the East to pay homage to the new born infant. They will be carrying gifts and will pay homage to this child."

Chris, to himself: *"This is interesting, but what has this got to do with me? Why are they interfering with what is essentially my area of influence?"*

"Chris be warned, your thoughts are not private. Everything you think and say in our presence is

176

FIRST CONTACT

projected directly to the command and control centre to which we are linked."

Chris cursed under his breath; he needed to be more careful!

"Even though you have your father and mother's memories and it would seem their psychic presence to guide you, you do not yet have the experience to proceed completely autonomously. This event in mankind's history is far too important to go unaided!"

"Fair enough! What would you have me do?" retorted *Chris* out loud.

"You will take the ATS and hover over the stable where the baby Jesus is born. You must be high enough that it will appear to all terrestrial beings that your ATS is a distant star. You will instruct your ATS to shine brightly to act as a guide for these three travellers heading to the barn in Bethlehem."

With that, the *Guardians* turn and leave the room, exiting the same way they entered, through a hole that appeared in the wall.

*

Stunned by the *Guardian's* lack of apparent interest in him, *Chris* watched the *Guardians* leave then walked back to where the *ATS* was stationed and entered the biomechanical entity.

177

"Bethlehem. Find the barn with baby Jesus in it and take me there."

The *ATS* shimmered...time and space appear as one...

Chris still finds the *ATS's* travelling silky sensation unnerving. *Krys* whispered in his mind to be calm; it's not the first time his father has travelled this way and will not be the last for *Chris*.

*

Mary was cradling the new born baby Jesus in her arms. All had not been so calm and serene a few hours before though.

Joseph, having helped deliver the baby boy was busy burning the bloodied rags on a small fire he had made just outside the stable. It was so kind of the farmer to let them stay here during the night.

They were within sight of Bethlehem when the cramps began short and sharp. She could not remember how far apart they were, but she *knew* the baby was on the way.

Joseph had run up to the farm house and banged on the house's door. He had begged the farmer to take them in to the house so Mary could give birth to the child under the farmer's roof.

At first the farmer had refused, but then seeing the state that Mary was in gave Joseph a bunch of rags, soap and a bucket of water and sent them to the barn.

Poor Joseph, he was beside himself with worry when she started screaming with the pain of labour. Luckily for Mary though Joseph knew what to do this time having overseen two of his sons' births from his first, late wife. Soon Mary had given birth to baby Jesus and all was calm in the stable once again.

*

Over the following years in Bethlehem, work for Joseph became scarcer and scarcer. The Romans were slowing down on the breaking down of doors, oxen yokes last many years without being replaced and the odd table and chair that he had been commissioned to make were few and far in-between.

After speaking to Mary, they both agreed that Joseph should return to their old home in Nazareth to pick up his old job as a carpenter there. Once established he would send for Mary and baby Jesus.

Jacob, Mary's father, had moved into their old house after buying it from them a few months previous. He continued to send them money every week as payment for the house, but the money was not enough to keep them and the baby housed and fed

179

in Bethlehem, the price of everything being that much more than in Nazareth.

When Joseph had not returned to Nazareth after being registered with the Roman census, the position of head carpenter had been given to Jacob.

With the building of Tsipori after the Romans had sacked the old town looking for Jewish rebels, Jacob had established a thriving construction business in Nazareth. Jacob was the main supplier of tradesmen and materials for the many construction projects. Now he subcontracted out many of the physical jobs. Subbing the work out was far more profitable than doing the work himself.

As luck would have it, the Roman census man came to Nazareth a few weeks after Mary and Joseph had left to go and get registered in Bethlehem. Jacob, knowing the requirements to ensure that he received a contract for the construction of Tsipori, was one of the first to be registered in Nazareth.

With his new-found wealth and profitable company, Jacob offered Joseph a good position as his chief carpenter, similar to the one he had left behind when he went to go and register himself and Mary in Bethlehem.

The money too was good, and to refuse the position would be an insult to his father-in-law. Also, it

FIRST CONTACT

was not that far away. Joseph could return to Bethlehem every ten days if he used Jacob's horse.

Once he had enough money to start again Joseph would rent a small home in Nazareth and go to fetch Mary and Jesus back in Jerusalem.

*

Things were going well in Tsipori for Joseph. He was busy installing a door on a newly constructed home that was to be the new residence of a local textile merchant when the accident happened...

A loose stone fell from the scaffold above where he was working, an accident that should never have happened. The stone, twice the size of a man's head crushed his skull, death was instantaneous.

After the death of Joseph, Jacob pleaded with Mary to return to Nazareth on many occasions; eventually he stopped asking and even threatened to cut off her allowance. She still refused to join him back in Nazareth, so he continued to send her the house money to help ease her care for herself and Jesus.

*

Twelve years went by when *Chris* was summoned again by the *Guardians*, this time to find a way of getting Mary and family out of Jerusalem. The now mad king Herod was determined to wipe out any

181

opposition to his immediate and future dynasty by killing the first born of every household in Jerusalem.

The reason for this mass blood bath was apparently due to an event that unfolded during one of his many night terrors. This only heightened his sense of paranoia and pushed his fragile mind over that very fine edge into the abyss from which there was no recovery.

Chris wondered if the *Guardians* had been meddling in his affairs again!
"This meddling must stop as it is my area of influence and all my plans are being ruined!" said *Chris* angrily.

Twenty-one years later, the Romans crucified Jesus on a hill, setting off a chain of events that would eventually change the course of Roman and mankind's history *forever!*

*

ROME

CIVIL

WAR

FIRST CONTACT

Chapter Fourteen

300 AD
Earth
Rome

Emperor Maximian was standing at the edge of his classical garden. He had ensured that the statues of his predecessors have been placed strategically around the garden for maximum effect. All who visit this wonderful garden could not fail to see his proud heritage.

Water played melodically as it ran down the steps leading from the private baths and into the garden pools. Maximian found the flow of water as it travelled down the steps particularly soothing, almost entrancing. Something disturbed his peaceful thoughts though...there was a smell of wood burning fragrantly in the air.

"This will not be tolerated!" exclaimed Maximian.

He will instruct the Domina, his wife, to beat the slave responsible for this intrusion to his olfactory senses during his evening time of contemplation.

How was he supposed to entertain the wealthy and influential if they failed to smell the roses he had imported from that barbaric land to the West,

"Britannia, I think it's called," said Maximian.

He was the first to have those thorny red beauties grace his home and if he can hold on to his position as Emperor, will be the only one to have them.

The problem with wild untamed plants though, is that they just do not respect authority. Already he had seen some roses growing in the nearby streets. He had given strict instructions to any slave running errands that they are to be removed when found and brought to him for disposal.

There were always games of political status and alliances being made. He had found it necessary to employ an army of informants; his spies were everywhere, but so were Constantine's.

"There will have to be a reckoning between the two of us one of these days," mused Maximian.

Luckily, he has a few distractions to look forward too when not embroiled in this game of deception. The old ways have returned, much to his *pleasure and delight*!

"Sins of the flesh really make life worthwhile. It defines who is noble is and who is not! There's nothing like swatting out that flickering candle like flame of a slave's life with a mere snap of the fingers. It makes me feel euphoric, it's intoxicating. Besides, they need to know who's in charge. *All will kneel before me!"*

His position as Emperor and subsequent rise to power was not completely of his own making this time

185

though. He had his son's manipulation and deception to thank for that...

His son, Maxentius, had orchestrated Maximian's rise to the position of Emperor, but true to the nature of the political game was only looking after his own interests. He was securing his right to rule when the old man died or was assassinated...

It had worked out quite well though; Maximian attended the state functions, feasts and orgies, dealt with the senate, while Maxentius rooted out any who opposed them.

When Maxentius found them through the family's many sources, he was ruthless, he had become quite adept at subduing their enemies, destroying them first politically, then physically.

"I taught him well!"

Bribery, blackmail, physical threat, marriage of enemies to allies, whatever it took to get a turn coat and then use them to ensure the family legacy!

"The end really does justify the means!" thought Maximian.

Going back to the old gods really had befitted their cause; all the blood and sacrifices, virgin deflowering, Maximian loved it all. He left the old hags to the other drunken old men;

"Any port in a drunken storm! Ha, not for me, only the youngest and purist shall I take!"

186

Maxentius even has an army of witches, soothsayers and witch doctors that can be used to read the *"future"* as he instructed the *"future"* to be. If the oracles did not favour what he wanted the senate, and of course his legions, to hear, then he could always rely on the witches and soothsayers to foretell what he wanted those in positions of power and influence to believe in and subsequently act on.

Statistically speaking, always ask the right questions of the right people!

Bribery was also a great tool, but had its limitations... But if the gods willed it, then that was a far more powerful mechanism with which to win over the hearts and minds of his armies' legions. The men were superstitious and believe in their god and omens. Tug on those beliefs and they will die for them and subsequently him.

Well he would give them what they wanted to hear...as long as it strengthened his political position.

"The problem with bribery or any form of persuasion is the cost; they keep on getting greedier and greedier with each year that passes. *Damn them!*"

Getting extra funds was always a problem; at least there were always the extra levies and taxes he could squeeze from of the outer provinces. Hispania was a great contributor to his noble cause. He chuckled to himself again,

187

"Noble cause...Ha!

I suppose self enrichment and power are noble causes!"

That Constantine though was a constant thorn in his side,

"The man acts like he's a descendant from Caesar Octavius himself. Trying to get family morals back on the table! *Bah...nicety is for the weak!*

*Nice guys always finish last, a*s the saying goes!"

Rome has rarely been a peaceful environment in which to raise one's offspring; it has had its share of slave rebellions, assassinations, wars, emperors, senates and republics vying for power, always bloody in some form or another.

"Not enough fear exists today. Give a slave the opportunity to become a free man, *and he thinks he has the right to be a noble*! Then there are the Christians, a pesky religious sect. They grow in strength and numbers everyday even though I have outlawed their worship of a single deity. Surely the threat of being the main attraction at the games would scare them into submission! I mean, there's nothing like a bit of flogging to get the scent of blood in the air and then releasing the hungry lions and hyenas to tear them apart. *That alone should have sent them scattered and broken into the abyss!"* exclaimed Maximian to himself.

188

FIRST CONTACT

"Again and again, hundreds of them digested and tortured, that should have dealt with the Christian scourge, but it just made them more determined!

Like the Jews though, they continue to stick to their faith! In times of persecution they simply go underground. People seem inspired by their sacrifice and their stubborn resolve. That it is better to die than to renounce their faith. Indeed, death they say is not the end for them. *Go figure!*"

Both the Jewish and Christian faiths keep getting stronger; *Chris* had to admire their resolve. In the past, the catacombs were where any persecuted group residing in Rome had taken refuge. The catacombs were now so extensive that no one knew where they began and where they ended.

"Send a few rat catchers in there," he chuckled at his own personal joke, "to catch those religious rodents and they all come back raving mad or worse, *converted*!

This will not do!"

If Maximian had his own way, he'd invoke the wrath of Hades. He would claim that the tunnels had ventured too deep and too close to the fires of Hades. So, to keep the fires of hell at bay, he would get his engineers to flood the tunnels and,

"KILL THEM ALL! HA... HA"

189

FIRST CONTACT

When he raised this option at one of the many orgies he had attended, *all for the state's benefit of course*, there was a bit of an *outcry!*

The mob would revolt, revolting creatures that they were, the senators had family ancestry buried down there, and it went *on* and *on!*

The one comment that held his attention though was from a so-called civil engineer with white hair and beard, hair not being very common as one gets older.

"What was his name?" *Chris* Stormbiggie or something...

"Not a proper Roman name that's for sure.

These fair-haired northerners have infiltrated all levels of Roman society – something would have to be done about that as well!" said Maximian out loud.

Anyway, this Chris was concerned that if the catacombs were flooded then Rome itself would collapse into the sinkholes that would be created. He stated, with some enthusiasm, that when the tunnels and caverns collapsed all of us would be sent into the fires of Hades!

What would be left of Rome would contaminate the drinking water when the Cloacae Maxima or sewers broke and spilled into the aqueduct system running under the city.

That was not what Maximian wanted...

FIRST CONTACT

Life at the moment was way too enjoyable to have it cut short just because he wanted to kill a few pesky Christians.

Maximian's thoughts drifted back to a few nights previous, a freshly captured Germanic slave girl, still a virgin, he was told!

"Well at least she screamed like a virgin! Ha ha!

One can never tell these days, it's amazing what people will pretend to be for a price!"

It was starting to get dark and his stomach was making hungry grumbling noises. Turning to face his Palacium, he started towards the lit porch where he knew there would be wine and meat prepared for him to gorge himself on.

The sun was just setting, a nice blood red.

"Soon it will be March again, and then it will be time to gather the troops and deal with that pesky Constantine,"

Maximian had taken two steps towards the villa when he heard a rustling noise emanating from one of the bushes that he had just sauntered past. Startled by the sound, he spun around just in time to see one of his hired henchmen subdue the would-be assassin. His man pulled out a cudgel and proceeded to bash the intruder until the man lay sprawled on the paving unconscious and bleeding but still alive as per his

FIRST CONTACT

instruction. All spies and assassins must be interrogated...

"*Supper first,* then the Domina can have her evil way with him," said Maximian to the henchman.

Sometimes she scared even him! The things she did to them was sadistic and inhuman; she had some kind of unnatural thirst for blood! He had not witnessed her bathing in their blood yet, but the rumour of her doing so was enough for him and very believable. Maximian felt a shiver run down his spine at the thought of his wife bathing in all her victims' blood.

Contemplating the would-be assassins' fate, Maximian continued on his way towards the Palacium.

"*Still...A message must be sent to the family that hired the would-be assassin!*" he hissed between his teeth.

Maximian quickly entered the Palacium trying not to look over his shoulder. Olive oil lamps burn, scattered haphazardly about the veranda, trying but failing to banish the shadows that lurk in every corner.

"*MORE LAMPS!*" commanded Maximian.

Slaves scurry to do his bidding; six more lamps are strategically placed and the darkness in the corners dissipates.

192

His wife was sitting at the table, glaring at him, *again!* Will she ever look at him with those doting loving eyes again...he thinks not.

Once he had even loved her, but now he just uses her to run the household and ensure his security. He was sure she uses that Jewish head of the guard for her sexual exploits...better the security man than him though.

"Well, loyalty at any cost then, it is definitely working! Ten spies and assassins in the past three months, must be some kind of record that. Constantine must be planning something big!" thought Maximian.

As he sat down, the first course of lentil soup was brought to the table. As was the custom in these treacherous times, the slave who brings it must taste it! Poison is another of the favourite ways to remove nobles competing for the right to rule Rome.

The slave girl, a plump girl taken from Britannia with ample breasts that almost dipped into the soup bowl, brought a wooden spoon full of the nutritious broth to her ripe rose-coloured lips.

He sometimes wondered if she got backache from those huge sacks on her chest, then dismissed the thought,

"Who cares!"

FIRST CONTACT

The tradition was to wait while the bard completed a song, normally about some battle resulting in the death of an emperor by poison or assassination.

"Julius Caesar's death in the senate was a good one! Let that be a lesson on friendship!" said Maximian, mockery in his tone.

"Trust no one is my motto," said Maximian, "*and I'm still alive!*"

Towards the end of the song, the fat Britannic girl was starting to sweat. Soon she was shivering and shaking, foaming at the mouth...then she collapsed in a heap at the foot of the table.

The Domina jumped to her feet, in the process knocking the table's contents to the floor.

"*BAR ALL THE DOORS NOW! NO-ONE GETS IN OR OUT! I WANT THE WOULD-BE POISONER CAUGHT!*

WHEN YOU FIND HER TAKE BOTH THE ASSASSIN AND POISONER TO THE CELLAR!" shouted the Domina.

Then smiling sweetly to her husband as if nothing had happened she snapped her fingers,

"Bring another meal! Cheese and fruit make sure it's untouched by anyone. Oh...and get rid of this dead slave girl. Bring me another."

*

After a few goblets of full-strength Adriatic wine, some figs and cheese, Maximian, feeling sufficiently numb prepared to venture down to the cellar. He dreaded watching the Domina apply her tortuous trade to the hapless victims. What made it worse was how much she seemed to enjoy inflicting pain on any who crossed swords with her. He felt her cold icy fingers run up his spine; he shuddered again unable to control his emotions.

Maximian grabbed another goblet of wine, drained its contents in one long gulp, and then proceeded down to the cellar.

Both assassins, captured and bound, were taken to the cellar where both traitors were stripped naked and hung from one of the rafters, toes barely touching the floor.

The naked girl was being beaten and sodomised as he walked in, her face was cut, and she was bleeding from the deep dark wounds caused by the whipping she had received. Her back and chest are a bloodied mess of ragged raw meat. The torn strips of flesh hang down in strips where the flogger had been particularly enthusiastic.

Not sure if she was conscious or not, the Domina instructs for the girl to be roused with a bucket of urine.

The girl screamed as the ureic acid bit into her wounds. It was then that Maximian noticed the fish shaped design tattooed on her ankle...*A Christian*!

195

"*How was she not noticed?*" Maximian asked his wife.

He had given strict instructions not to employ them as it was well known that Constantine used many of them as spies and servants.

Constantine was even known to be sympathetic to their cause and may even have started the campaign to make their worship legal,

"*You know that Constantine hires Christians, they even walk the streets openly displaying their miniature crucifixes!*" exclaimed Maximian. If he wasn't so concerned with his own safety, the tone in his voice would have been many octaves higher.

The girl was now fully awake. Maximian drew a hidden dagger from his robe and proceeded to cut out her left kidney.

He did not need to find out who her master was, he already knew. The Christian girl screamed, a hoarse pitiful gurgle emits from her throat, and then she passed out, sinking into that haven of the dark painless abyss.

The thick black blood sprayed all over the straw covered floor and muddied his tunic. Maximian's hands were covered in the foul stuff.

The Domina turned hands on hip and stared venomously at Maximian.

FIRST CONTACT

"You've just stopped my fun! I wanted to remove a couple more fingers on her ugly calloused hands before letting her fall into the abyss."

Maximian, turned to his wife,

"I know that she works for Constantine! There is no need to inflect any more suffering on this piece of godless trash!" retorted Maximian.

"Husband, you know as well as I do, that without a witnessed confession we cannot accuse anyone! Even if one knows who sent the unfortunate messenger, we need a confession," replied the Domina calmly, her voice dripping honey.

Maximian pulled out his dagger again and slit the girl's throat ending her life. Even he could not bear to see any more cruelty inflicted on the young girl.

"Now look what you've done!" screamed the Domina.

"Now we'll have to start all over again with the would-be boy assassin!"

The boy, having long since dropped the contents of his bowels, started to beg for mercy.

"Please... Please! I will confess to everything if only for a quick death!" pleaded the young man.

"Confess then and you will be rewarded with a quick death," said the Domina to the young terrified boy.

197

The petrified boy pleaded guilty to working for Constantine and then signed the parchment placed in front of him. As promised the boy had his head removed in one swift slashing movement by the Jewish mercenary.

Satisfied, the Domina turned to join her husband who was just about to leave the cellar. Following him, two steps behind as was her place, they both started to ascend the stairs.

Just before they were out of earshot, she turned back to her Jewish henchman,
"Dispose of the bodies discretely, and clean the floor,"

Humming a tune as they left the cellar, the Domina, with a sated smile on her lips started to ask Maximian how his day had been.

*

Chris had been in Rome for a few months now; he had managed to rent a villa and hire a few servants. Money comes when he needed it. Somehow the *Guardians* always got their hands on whatever he needed.

He had been observing the two opposing noble factions, one under Maximian and the other lead by Constantine. *Chris* was backing the Christian supporter Constantine.

198

FIRST CONTACT

He had been in constant contact with Constantine and appeared to have gained the confidence and trust of the man who wanted to bring back piety to the Roman way of life.

Chris had presented himself as a well-established civil engineer from one of the northern territories. He had already made an impact on the Roman architects; now he was pressing them on the need for greater hygiene design in their town layout. *Design health by architectural layout so to speak!* He urged them to plan for more open spaces, so the people would be able to exercise regularly to get healthy and as a benefit of the exercise expel their ailments as they got fitter. After all, a healthy body leads to a healthy mind.

He had convinced Constantine that the wind from the river would blow away the bad aliments that cause diseases such as plague and dysentery if the city was planned correctly. There was also to be a ban on killing felines as they could keep the rat population under control, another source of disease.

Constantine's fondness for family values brought him daily into contact with both the Jewish and Christian leaders. He employed many of them on his staff as servants, not slaves, and listened to their elderly wise leaders in matters concerning the way they ruled their own people. In doing so Constantine hoped

199

to gain from their knowledge and experience and to rule Rome wisely when he eventually became Emperor.

The only dark cloud on *Chris's* horizon was which religion he should back and press Constantine to follow.

"Should he back the Jewish people with their utter belief in their faith and family values, or the Christians' with similar values but with a newer single God?"

The choice was making him experience a feeling of uncertainty, one that he had rarely encountered in the past.

During one of their informal suppers *Chris* raised the question with Constantine,

"The Jewish and Christian faiths are becoming more and more accepted by the people of Rome with every day that passes. It may be prudent to align your house with one or even both of them," *Chris* casually mentioned whilst stuffing a fig into his mouth.

"I have been thinking about that very idea my friend but have not yet made up my mind. Oh, I'd prefer to align with both faiths, but history has taught Rome that to be divided is to be conquered...

According to my spies in his household, Maximian intends to engage me in battle next March. I have sent messengers to request an audience with the oracle, but she will not even agree to meet me. I believe that Maximian has already greased her palm with silver!" A frown creased Constantine's brow as he wondered how to overcome this political obstacle.

"Have you thought about approaching the Christian leaders for advice?" asked *Chris*.

"No, but that is another option, good idea. I will summon the head priest immediately,"

Constantine made his wishes known and thirty minutes later the summoned priest appeared as if by magic at the Palacium gates and was ushered inside. After a few escorted minutes, the Christian leader had arrived on the veranda where *Chris* and Constantine were lounging.

Constantine gestured for the priest to sit down on one of the loungers opposite himself.

"Tell me priest, what is your name?"

"Peter...sir."

"Aah, Peter...Is that a normal Christian name?"

"It is my lord,"

"Peter...I have a small issue with one of my many ill wishers. And as you know; I have always been supportive of your way of life. I have even lobbied in the senate on your behalf to make the worship of a single deity legal. This in itself is one of the main reasons that a certain noble house is plotting against me. So...I believe it is time for you and your God to aid me in my quest to legitimise your religion. And if I am made Emperor I will make sure that Christianity is no

201

longer outlawed. So, will your God protect me and send me from the field of battle with Maximian victorious?"

"Sir...The only way that will occur is if you swear fealty to the Lord God and no other false gods, then it will be made so," replied Peter.

Constantine stretched out on his lounger; reaching for a plump fig he squeezed the base of the sweet fruit until the soft mashed contents burst into his mouth. Pondering this ultimatum for a moment,

"Besides its only words and if I emerge victorious, then I might take this Christian God seriously. But if I lose then I know Christianity was the wrong choice. Then there's always the Jews," thought Constantine, and then nodded his head in agreement, "I agree...I will swear fealty to your God."

Peter eased himself out of the lounger and stood upright in front of where he had been sitting. Instructing Constantine to kneel in front of him, to which the noble and powerful Roman reluctantly complied. Peter then removed a vial of holy oil from the confines of his robes. *Chris,* seeing that Constantine had made his choice, smiled, as he too now knew which religion to put his energy and resources behind. *Chris* then excused himself from the small gathering and walked back into the Palacium's interior. As he left the Roman villa he could hear the priest chanting the Latin-based prayers for the swearing in ceremony and conversion to Christianity that was about to begin.

*

The battle with Maximian goes as the priest had foretold; Constantine entered Rome like a conquering hero. The thought never entered his mind that he had just put to the sword thousands of his fellow Roman citizens. Brother slew brother, father maimed son; but loyalty to the Legion was all that mattered.

The festivities that followed the carnage were debaucherous...more pagan than Christian. Peter, watching the horde of human bodies revel in gluttony and sexual pleasure soon realised that Constantine had used him to get his soldiers morale up and had not truly converted to Christianity, not in the smallest capacity at all.

A few weeks later Constantine was inaugurated as ruler of Rome, more feasting and debauchery occurred as the Roman citizens celebrated the end to the feud between the two mightiest of houses. There was so much physical excess that gluttony could only be considered as one of the minor crimes that was being committed during the celebrations.

Constantine awoke bleary eyed one morning after an exceptional night of debauchery and kicked the

203

slave girl lying next to him. He barely remembered ploughing that field last night. The girl did not budge; kicking her again he tried to remove her from his bed.

"Man...what a headache!"

Constantine thought about calling the surgeon so he could trepan a hole in his skull and let the bad spirits out that where causing this awful pain in his head. Wincing as he shook his head from side to side trying to shake out the evil spirits, he grabbed the half empty wine goblet next to the bed and downed the contents.

"*Yuk!*" he exclaimed as he spat out a large dead black fly that had drowned in the stale wine.

It was only then that he noticed the girl lying next to him was dead. It looked like she must have been strangled while he slept. Her eyes bulged out of her eye sockets and there was a red ring around her neck that was slowly turning a dark black. A note protruded from the corner of her mouth.

Prying the piece of parchment from between the dead girls lips he started to read,

"Meet me on the battle field...You slimy scum!

Then I will show you what mercy really is when you fall defeated by my powerful left sword arm. I will cleave you in two and show you how a mighty warrior treats his enemies. You should not have spared my life you weak minded weasel. Your entire family will be

ruined and shamed, the crows will feast on their bloated ravished bodies!"

Maxentius

"MERCY...MERCY!" shouted Constantine spittle spraying the air as he flew into a rage.
"I'LL SHOW YOU MERCY!
WHAT AN INSULT!
IF I DIE, IT WILL BE IN BATTLE OR NOT AT ALL."
With shaking hands, partly from drink, partly from rage, Constantine dressed himself as quickly as his fumbling hands could manage. He was still shaking with rage when he stormed out of the bedroom.

*

As soon as the news of Constantine's victory over Maximian at the battle of Milvian Bridge had reached Maxentius, Maximian's son, the boy had fled Rome before Constantine had had a chance to sever the boys head from his shoulders. Maxentius had fled west to Hispania and taken his loyal troops with him.

Their loyalty was mainly based on his ability to pay them from the large purse of taxes he had levied out of the local populous. Now as the word had spread of his generosity, Maxentius had under his command at least fifteen legions all loyal to him or to his money at least.

205

FIRST CONTACT

Maxentius, thirsting for revenge for the killing of his father Maximian, had issued several challenges and insults to Constantine trying to goad him into another battle. *So* far Constantine had ignored them, but this last insult went too far, honour and family pride were now at stake. If Constantine let the insults continue without a response, then the people of Rome would lose their respect for him and reject him as ruler of Rome. This could lead to the mob rioting, Rome would burn, and he would hang. That would make it easy for Maxentius to simply march into Rome and claim a victory for the people.

Constantine could only muster ten legions to Maxentius's fifteen legions. As numbers meant everything, this could end very poorly for him and his family.

"What to do?" wondered Constantine.

"Where is that damn engineer, what's his name again?" A badly throbbing head clouded his memory. The engineer always seems to have such good advice. He must get him to come and stay at the Palacium. Better to have him close by than allow him to be corrupted by one of his enemies. Worse yet he could have been taken in by Maxentius.

Then it came to him! Call that priest Peter of the Christians again, surely, he will forgive him and help out with the numbers dilemma.   Constantine shouted for the priest to be brought before him.

The next day Peter arrived at Constantine's Palacium, wary of what the Emperor would say, or for that matter demand. The last time Constantine had taken him for a fool,

"That will not happen again!" said Peter in a determined tone.

"If he wants my blessing for the upcoming battle with Maxentius then he will have to be baptised! I will not compromise on this."

Fortunately, Queen Helena, Constantine's wife, had already converted to Christianity. At every opportunity she would whisper in his ear that he must convert to Christianity, so his soul could be saved; eventually she would wear him down. She had tried using every feminine trick she had learnt during her many years as Constantine's Domina, always a touch here, and a hint of something forbidden every so often, but mostly she had tried to appeal to him on an intellectual level. For a man who had everything, the only thing left was immortality and that she assured him could only be obtained in the Kingdom of Heaven.

Constantine, recently dressed after a restless night, was sporting a white toga. Dribble stains marked the torso portion of the white garment from when he had hastily shovelled some bread and olives down his throat just a few minutes before Peter had arrived.

He indicated for Peter to take a seat opposite him on the veranda. Constantine, remembering the victorious outcome of the previous battle with Maximian, recalled that some of his soldiers were now sporting a new symbol on their shields.

"What was that symbol?" He racked his memory, a letter *'P'*, *"Was that to symbolise Peter and their Christian God? It also had a rotated cross on it...Right that was it! A diagonal cross and the letter 'P',"* Constantine looked up at the priest and an idea leapt to his mind,

"Peter...I have been mulling this over in my mind for some time now and have started to see the error in my pagan ways...So as token of my sincerity I wish to be baptised. If you agree...I will instruct my legions to paint the Christian symbol on all their shields. Every soldier will appear to be fighting for your God and now mine," Constantine paused letting his proposal etch its way into Peter's mind.

"If I am victorious, I will ban all other religions throughout the Roman empire, making Christianity the only religion of choice," Constantine continued.

Peter, taken aback by the sudden change of heart, thought that God must be working through Helena for this is exactly what he had hoped for. She had, after

208

all, been constantly egging him on about converting to Christianity.

Peter nodded his agreement and then ordered his companion to bring him a large copper bowl so he may perform the baptism.

"I agree Constantine...I will baptise you and confirm that you are a Christian, but only if you truly believe in the Christian God,"

"I believe," said Constantine, doubt creaking into his mind.

Chris, who was standing on the veranda cloaked, observed the conversation and subsequent baptism, wondered how he could encourage the unification of the Roman Empire under the Christians. The more unified the greatest Empire on the planet became the closer he would be to achieving his goal of a unified mankind before the *Xhoseti* arrive. He left the veranda, made his way through the atrium with its shallow pool and exited the Roman Palacium back onto the streets of Rome. Not stopping to get involved in any of the many atrocities he barely managed to avoid, *Chris* left Rome and went straight to the *ATS* to see how he could aid Constantine when the battle took place.

A few days later, on the field of *Mars* just outside the gates of Rome, the two Roman armies' face up to one another, take formation and prepare for battle. The precision of their tactical formations and the speed at which the commands were issued and subsequently employed never ceased to impress *Chris* who was floating cloaked in the *ATS* above the battlefield.

Tactics aside, the only thing that really counted when both sides were equally well trained was the number of swords that each general commanded. Both Constantine and Maxentius had been schooled by the same tutors, had the same military backgrounds and Roman upbringing, deception was in their blood. Tactical advantage would be paid for in blood and the price would be high for both sides no matter the victor.

Maxentius had the advantage though, two hundred and fifty thousand soldiers to Constantine's forty thousand. *Chris* has a plan to even the odds though and hopes that he can turn the battle so it favours Constantine and the Christian soldiers.

Chris had flown the cloaked *ATS* midway between the two silently waiting armies. Nothing but the occasional clang of steel on armour banding could be heard across the plain of *Mars* as the wind rocked the occasional spear loose and onto someone's armour. Even the ravens were silent as they waited for the carnage to begin.

Chris instructed the *ATS* to take a snapshot of the symbol of Saint Peter on one of the soldier's shields; he then instructed the *ATS* to project the symbol shrouded in bright white light towards Maxentius's waiting legions. The brightly shining Christian cross had the effect of temporarily blinding Maxentius's soldiers, panicking the blinded men who uncertainly raised their shields to cover their eyes.

Chris, seeing the effect the blinding light had on Maxentiu's army, directed the same symbol as a golden cross towards Constantine's troops making sure his troops were not blinded by the golden light but rather so they saw it as a symbol of hope and enlightenment.

The golden cross of Peter gave new hope to Constantine's outnumbered but highly trained army. Taking the sign of the cross as one of divine intervention from heaven, Constantine gives the order to attack Maxentius's troops. The Christian soldiers let out a mighty roar and to the sound of trumpet blowing start forward with the order and precision of a highly trained Roman single cohort and start the attack.

Constantine's troops, expecting their opponent to start towards them in typical Roman fashion and orderly formation, find that while their opposition is being blinded by the symbol in the sky, they have not moved! Confusion reigns amongst the ranks of Maxentius's legions; it's as if the soldiers were filled with the first-time jitters of an initiate...none move! No orders were issued, no defences were formed...they just stood there dumbfounded, like deer caught in the

211

beam of a bright light. The blinded soldiers stand uncertainly, shifting from one foot to another holding up their shields protecting their eyes and awaiting instruction. By now Constantine's army had snuck up to their held high shield wall and could see the men with their exposed bellies. The battle was short, as soon as the stabbing started many of Maxentius's soldiers changed sides almost instantaneously. The first of the converted soldiers took to painting the sign of the cross on their shields with anything at hand, even the blood of their fallen comrades and joined Constantine's army. Within hours the two armies had merged into one much larger army and in so doing had created an almighty, now Christian, Roman army under the soon to be crowned Emperor, Constantine.

*

Later that night, while Maxentius, now tied to a tree and wallowing in self-pity at his latest misfortune, a cloaked *Chris* crept up to the *defeated,* once mighty general and cuts his bonds. He leaves the knife on the ground where Maxentius could see it.

A guard, seeing that Maxentius had slipped his bonds and was free, shouted out the alarm, drew his sword and rushed towards Maxentius, eager for the reward that must surely follow the recapture of this would be tyrant.

212

Maxentius side stepped the over-eager rushing soldier, and with a quick downward strike slashed through his neck. The guard went down clutching the gaping wound in his neck...Choking on his own blood the young man still had thoughts of the reward he should have received gleaming in his eyes. It stayed there right up to the very last moment until they glazed over, and he fell to the ground, dead.

Maxentius then turned, knowing that his only chance of survival would be to run for the woods...run so he could return and fight another day, but it was too late!

The now dead soldier had alerted the rest of the camp and within moments four more experienced legionaries had now surrounded him. Knowing that his end would be humiliating and torturous, Maxentius turned the knife's sharp blade on himself and proceeded to thrust the blade deep and hard into his heart. A few minutes later the light started to fade from Maxentius's eyes, then the eyes started to glaze over, turning to dark obsidian lifeless stone.

And then Maxentius was no more.

*

Back in Rome, Queen Helena, wife to the self-declared *Constantine the Great,* was readying her huge train of servants and other worldly goods for her

213

FIRST CONTACT

journey to the Holy Land. Much good work had to be completed and time was running out. Helena was not going to waste any more time before spreading the greatness of Christianity.

"I think the first church I shall construct will be The Church of the Nativity in Bethlehem," Helena said to her maid servant.

"Constantine can rule Rome, I have more important work to do!" and with that she gave the command for her troop to make for the docks where her boats were berthed, waiting to take her to the Holy Land.

*

Chris smiled to himself.

"Finally, some progress!"

Mankind was at last on the path to mental cohesion; his father would be proud. With that he can feel his mother rubbing the back of his neck and his father giving him a fatherly pat on the back.

"Well done my son...Very subtle, not interfering until the last moment, a slight push here and there, couldn't have done it better myself" whispered *Krys* in *Chris's* head.

Swelling with a sense of accomplishment, *Chris* then instructed the *ATS*;

"Mexico...Take me there,"

Time and space seem as one, then that now familiar silky feeling...

*

MEXICO

FIRST CONTACT

Chapter Fifteen

500 AD:
Earth
Mexico

Chris mentally projects,
"*Jaguar*"
The ATS morphed into the shape of a large black cat...make that the largest feline to ever walk the planet.
"*Cloak*"
The *ATS* fades into the jungle.
"*Chichen Itza co-ordinates?*"
The longitude and latitude appear in his mind.
"*Take me there,*"
The ATS in the form of an invisible jaguar stealthily started to walk forward, slowly at first, one paw in front of the other, then with what appeared to be growing confidence the biomechanical entity started to jog. Within seconds the *ATS* started to run the sleek predatory charge of a hunting cat eager to close in on its victim.

The *ATS* seemed oblivious to the dense vegetation, almost cutting a path through it as it passed the space in which it has just been. The jungle vegetation then appeared to fold back into its former position just as

217

soon as the biomechanical entity had glided through it. Time and space appear to shimmer around the *ATS*.

*

Miguel was worried about his rite of passage ceremony; still he knew that it will be worth it and the pain would soon be over...well that was what his mother had told him. He will try to not scream during the painful preparation for his rite of passage through which he will become accepted as a man of the tribe and be treated as an equal amongst them.

The fire ants that the *Shaman* would make sting the initiate could kill if the intended recipient had not undergone the preparation inoculations before the main ceremony. The stings were administered in small doses so the human body could build up a resistance to the venom. If the initiate did not have this resistance to the venom, they would die if attacked by the fire ants in any great quantity for the first time.

Miguel squatted down in the low shrubbery, aiming for the small hole he had dug just moments before with a now discarded branch of one of the local jungle saplings. While he waited horrific images and possible painful outcomes of the ceremony he will have to undergo later, flooded his already over active mind. He winced at the thought of the fire ant's stings that he had received previously at the hands of the Shaman.

Done with his ablutions, he grabbed a handful of nearby leaves and continued with his morning cleansing ritual.

This morning though, he had ventured deeper than normal into the jungle, not too far though...he could still see the earthen mound ramparts where the new water storage dam was being built.

His mother insisted that he must perform these basic cleansing rituals every day if he wanted to grow up strong like his father and also have strong children of his own. It was then that he heard a rustling noise just over to his right shoulder.

Instinctively Miguel lay down on the ground pretending to be a small unthreatening mouse, as still as a dead mouse. He lies so still that he can hear the whoosh of blood as it rushes through his highly sensitive ears. *Thump...Thump* banged his adolescent heart.

"Please lord Jaguar spare my pathetic tiny little life," as he waited, he mentally begged for the jungle god to spare him. But like all his tribe he knew that the jungle shows no mercy and he was ready to sacrifice himself to the lord Jaguar if that was the will of the gods. At least then he would be sent to the heavens so he could be with his ancestors.

Slowly he turned his head to where the noise had emanated from. Just through the dense vegetation he

219

FIRST CONTACT

could barely make out a shimmering jaguar-like shape starting to materialise. It appeared to be forming out of the air...then it was gone, and a white haired, white bearded old man dressed in a grey cloak stood in the place of where the unbelievable huge jaguar had been.

The stranger turned to Miguel and smiled at him; the old man's grey eyes shimmered and then putting his back to Miguel he turned away and continued his journey up to the incomplete dam and then onwards toward the small sacrificial temple that was being constructed. The construction sites bustled with activity even at this early hour of the morning.

*

A few years later, Techokahn, the high priest, placed the brightly coloured ceremonial helmet on his tanned but gleaming shaven head. Bright red and blue bird feathers spike out from the golden shining head piece making the priest seem alien and otherworldly. A brightly attired tropical figure of authority,

"Today is the day that the water canals will be finished," he whispered to himself.

What a marvel of civil engineering, when the flood gates are opened, control and supply of fresh water will never be a problem for his people again! The great flood plain where the vaulted village stood on the flood stilts will be turned into a hydroponic garden providing

ROBERT J STEPHENS

an abundance of water grown edible plants, fish and crustaceans.

His thoughts were filled with hope and promise for the future prospects of his people and his family,

"They will never go hungry again! There is even a drinking dam for the jungle animals to visit, the lord of the jungle may even visit and enjoy some of the bounty that I have to offer. I will instruct the people to stay clear of this area throughout most of the year. The only exception will be during the winter months when the beasts would have no babies in their bellies," thought Techokahn.

Raising his arms in an arc he turned to the imaginary gathered villagers and then continued out loud,

"Each family is to be allocated one small animal per lunar cycle to feed themselves and their children. No more...no less! You the people of the jungle will need to understand the limits of your bounty and you must self regulate the hunting. *If you take too many animals they will move away and then the dam and canal digging will have been for nothing!"* said Techokahn, preparing his speech for later. He lowered his large muscled outstretched arms slowly as if already in front of the cheering crowd and asking them to be still.

Mankind has always enjoyed a destructive nature, and with it came an instinct to move into an area and

221

FIRST CONTACT

decimate the local wildlife and then simply move on, following and chasing their food source much as any predator would. Recently though some portions of mankind had started to farm their food and instead of gathering wild fruits and nuts, they had started to plant crops instead. In order to farm and form settlements they had to burn down the jungle trees to make a clearing, not understanding or even being concerned with the needs of the other animals that were in their way.

Techokahn knew that this slash and burn tactic must be stopped or his people would have no choice but to move on again as the land needed to replenish itself before it could become fertile again. This constant nomadic lifestyle must be brought to an end if they were to prosper and multiply.

The new water ways and hydroponic gardens should eliminate the need to move on again, for now... There would come a time when they would need to expand again, but for now the dam would suffice. With the increased supply of protein, the tribe's women would be able to have more children. Some of them would become male warriors and more warriors meant better protection against any invading locals. The dam and farms needed to be functional as soon as possible. Then and only then would he allow slash and burn clearing to be applied to the jungle again. That in turn will only be to make way for new floating gardens, or maybe even the growing of corn.

Techokahn had heard rumours of a people to the north that were growing their own corn and even planting roots that grow into edible tubers. He wanted to find out how to do the same, but messengers rarely got through to them. The journey seemed to get more perilous every year.

It was then that a young messenger came to get him. Still dressed in his full brightly coloured feathered regalia, Techokahn was led by one of his young warriors to where the stone weighted rope holding the massive wooden sluice gate waited for him in the manmade canal. All he had to do was cut the rope and the sluice gate would rise majestically then flood the downstream area of the blocked river canal and fill the dam. It was going to be an amazing sight.

"Very clever that man! Who was he, this *Chris* from the East?" A strange man with white hair and a white beard, with a strange name! He was very different to any of his own brown skinned warriors.

"He must be very hot in that long robe he always wore," He claimed to have come from over the sea from the east riding in the belly of a great fiery dragon. "Who can guess the will of the gods?" mumbled Techokahn to no one in particular.

223

All Techokahn knew was that without his help this magnificent project could not have been achieved. Sure, they had started the dam, but they had hoped that the rain water would fill it; that just did not happen, the water just drained away. *Chris* had taught them methods of sealing the base of the dam and then making the canal to fill the dam.

In fact, *Chris* was here now, holding the obsidian blade with which Techokahn will cut the rope.

Techokahn greets *Chris* with a slight nod of his head; a king of the Maya does not bow to any man, no matter how clever or important they may appear to be.

Chris hands him the blade, which Techokahn raises high above his head to the shouting and cheering of the crowd present.

With a slashing technique used so many times to decapitate his enemies, the rope is severed in two. The wooden gate rises slowly at first, then rapidly, rising the five meters and halting a few metres above the rushing whirling flow of murky canal water.

The water is dark and rich, full of minerals and nutrients for the fish and plants to thrive in.

He had been warned by Chris that twice a year the water garden, river and canals must be dredged. This was to avoid a build up of sediment on the bottom of the waterways which could flood the nearby areas where they have built a village. If they are not dredged, the river will rise and as it gets choked, the flow of water will rapidly increase thereby eroding the nearby embankments. Then the canal will burst its banks and flood everything in its path, destroying all they had achieved.

"There is an animal of great proportions in a land far to the southeast of here that could be used to clear the waterways. It is often referred to as a great sea cow in that far away land called Africa; I call it hippopotamus, as I have never seen one in the sea. They are used in Africa, to keep the rivers from getting choked by the local plants. The hippos walk along the bottom of the river, churning up the river bed ensuring that no plants take root and allow the water to flow.

Although you do not have a beast as majestic as the African hippo, there is a smaller version, a pygmy hippo if you will, that could be trained and used in a similar application to keep your waterways clear. It would be prudent to ensure that your hunters do not kill or trap them as well," *Chris* explained to Techokahn.

Later a great feast ensues; local animals from the jungle make up most of the menu. A few staples like ant eggs and locust legs are mixed with goat milk and cane sugar, then churned into a thick stodgy paste for all to gorge themselves on.

After sampling a particularly well-prepared leg of iguana, the skin nice and crunchy, it was time to prime

225

Techokahn as to the completion of the step-pyramid for this area as previously requested by the *Guardians*.

As per *Guardian* instruction, they should also build an observatory to view the celestial planets and star systems. The *Guardians* were extremely insistent about this single detail, something to do with a calendar and the cycle of life.

"I know there is a plain not far from here where the land is right for the building of a great pyramid. It can be used to worship the gods of the sky. *Chichen Itza* you should name it," stated *Chris* to Techokahn.

The Maya king turned to *Chris*,

"We as a nation are deeply indebted to you for what you have helped us achieve with the water works, but to build a pyramid of such grand proportions will require that we use immense resources," explained Techokahn.

"The jungle will have to be burnt down to make a clearing and men will have to be enslaved. There will be war with much pain and suffering. Why do you ask this of me?" queried Techokahn concern in his voice.

Chris was stuck. Everything the king said was true. They have peace and have provided for their future with the water garden, but if the pyramid did not get built then the weapon would not be completed, and man would perish in the war with the *Xhoseti* a few thousand years from now!

226

"King Techokahn, I would not ask this of you and your people if it was not of the utmost importance. You will have to be convinced that the pyramid must be built and in this case the end will justify the means.

Tonight, I will take you on a journey to convince you of my sincerity and the importance of this great project."

As twilight approached, *Chris* went to meet the king. When he arrived at the king's hut he found him partaking of a large quantity of beer and agave spirit.

Luckily the king had the constitution of a hippo and, although slightly intoxicated, could still command his presence with impressive authority.

"It is time to see the stars my king of the Maya!" *Chris* projected into Techokahn's mind,

"Follow me,"
Chris led the slightly unsteady king to the outskirts of the village where the *ATS* waited,

"Morph...Rocket ship with access for this humanoid. De-cloak!"

The space where the *ATS* waited shimmered and distorted and then an upright lookalike rocket propelled missile was standing awaiting the pleasure of Techokahn himself.

"With this vehicle, you shall travel to the stars and all will be revealed to you. You will discover why you

227

need to build the pyramid of Chichen Itza," explained *Chris* to the now much soberer king.

"Are you ready to see the future?"
Techokahn nods in the affirmative and the *ATS* morphs around his body.
Fake rocket flames appear at the base of the many faceted stepped shaped tubular rocket, a clear canopy encases the king and then with a roar the rocket blasts off up and into the sky, heading straight toward the *Guardian's* orbiting station.

"Chris to Guardians," he mentally projects.

"There is a Maya king on route to you who requires an indoctrination program to change his mind on building the step-pyramid at Chichen Itza. He will need some knowledge of the stars in the immediate solar system and some rudimentary knowledge of constellations," Chris paused for a moment almost enjoying his moment of control,

"You will also need to imprint in him the craving to create a zodiac calendar and for that an astrological viewing platform or observatory as you requested.

Please also impress on him the threat from the Xhoseti two thousand years from now. I do not believe the actual date of the invasion needs to be imparted to him," again paused almost childishly chuckling to himself,

"You have five hours before he will be missed."

"We hear you Chris," after a short pause, *"and will comply!"* a *Guardian* whispered in his mind, disdain evident in the manner the pause was delivered.

*

Six hours later the *ATS* in its natural tubular shape touched down close to where *Chris* was standing. The *ATS* extended its tube-like appendage and the king was expelled then left lying inert on the ground.

Chris picked him up, the Morph-Suit adapts, sending energy where needed so Techokahn felt as heavy as a small child. *Cloaked* and still carrying the king, he made his way back to the village and laid him on the floor of his bed chamber.

"No doubt he will awaken with a thick head from the festivities of yesterday. Then the memories of the night's travel will start to slowly return to him, and hopefully the building of *Chichen Itza* will soon begin," said *Chris* out loud.

Chris, still cloaked, left the slumbering king and walked back to the *ATS*.

*

Techokahn rouses and shakes his head; wincing he holds his head in his hands. A servant is standing nearby with water and fruit.

229

Gesturing to the servant for the water and fruit, he eats and drinks, then jumps up as if in shock.

"CALL THE HEAD OF THE GUARD...PREPARE FOR WAR!

WE NEED RECRUITS...A TEMPLE MUST BE BUILT!" he bellowed, wincing in the process.

Chris, hovering above the village notices the commotion and with a grimace, remembers his own voice saying,

"The end justifies the means!"
He instructs the *ATS* to take him to the *Atlantic* pyramid to await the *Guardians* summons.

A long-needed rest in the *ATS's* stasis chamber will be most welcome!

*

ROBERT J STEPHENS

PYRAMID
WEAPONS
MODULE

FIRST CONTACT

Chapter Sixteen

800 AD:
Weapon Activation
Earth

Chris, having been summoned by the *Guardians* to their station in orbit, was now standing in the centre of a large spherical room. The platform he stands on has one access point, an impossibly thin yet sturdy walkway. He expected the walkway to at least have some spring or resilience when he walked on it.

As he walked down the ramp to take his appointed position in the centre of the sphere nothing flexed, not even a murmur of movement. The material that the walkway was constructed from kept its molecular composition a complete mystery.

It must be made from some kind of carbon-based Nano-Tube morph technology. The bridge adds material where needed to take up any localised strain, much the same way his suit uses its morphing capabilities. The *Guardians* love of the dramatic never ceases to amuse him though...

With their overly large heads, heavy brow and elongated ears with a fish hook shaped curl to the nostril gave the impression of great mental prowess and power, '*deep in thought*', even wise, sprang to *Chris's* mind.

232

"Here I am...striving to ensure mankind's future and they're more concerned *with appearances*! Hence the dramatic, over emphasized head heavy black suits they wear!"

What *Chris* did not realise is that those *large headed black face dominant suits*, are in fact a complex life support system. They protect and sustain the cerebellums of the six men who gave up their physical bodies tens of thousands of years ago in order to concentrate their energies on this social experiment here on planet Earth.

Without the life support suits, they would have perished a long...long time ago.

The regeneration sacs in his *ATS* have revitalised and sustained him for the past eight hundred years, but he knows that the time will come when he too will go to meet the *Grand Architect of the Universe.*

The wall of the sphere shimmers and the *Guardians* make their dramatic entrance, filtering around to their allotted positions elevated just above him. No seating was visible, but then that was what *Chris* had expected, more drama! What a waste of resources.

They don't impress him...

"Chris, we have summoned you here to instruct you on how to install the defence system for the already

233

constructed pyramids," whispered a voice in *Chris's* head.

A set of images appears in his mind of the currently completed pyramids of Egypt, China, Atlantis and Japan. The access portals leading to a central rectangular opening deep inside the bowels of each pyramid is highlighted as glowing orange rectangular points.

"You will deliver, via the transport portal, the weapon's module to the central void in each of the pyramids. The basic module will then morph into the actual weapon using the resources of the pyramid itself. When sufficient material has been absorbed by the module, construction of the weapon itself will begin," informed the voice in his head.

"The pyramids of Atlantis and Japan, already having been constructed, have the weapon components already installed and are complete. However, only your genetic code will activate the weapon; fortunately, they are all linked so activating one will suffice to enable them all. These two pyramids have been placed under the ocean prior to this meeting. When submerging the Atlantean pyramid, a minor tsunami wave was unfortunately created.

Although submergence was completed in a controlled manner, the resulting wave swell was observed on the coasts of North America, Ireland and

234

Britain. The impact on these loosely populated areas had a minimal effect on the humans residing there, but local fauna and flora were destroyed. Many sea dwelling creatures were driven inland on the wave and were decimated when the water receded." the voice inside his head paused for a moment then continued,

"Unfortunately, when the pyramid of Japan was submerged there was significant damage to the local islands. This particular area suffered significant loss in human life as well as all other living creatures. Even the landscape was changed with the destructive power of the tsunami wave that ensued," explained the voice in his head.

"We fear that the pyramid has changed the environment sufficiently to accentuate any future environmental disasters that befall the area. We have engaged the internal sensors of each of the pyramids and only the Atlantis pyramid remains undamaged!

The pyramid off the coast of Japan has had the entrance portal destroyed. Fortunately, the weapon remains intact and can be activated remotely from any of the other working pyramids."

The voice in his head goes silent, *Chris* feels like some response is expected of him,

"Never the less, I shall go to Atlantis and verify that all is in working order. Too much is at stake!" replies *Chris* via the mind link.

"*The Easter Island pyramid has recently been constructed along with the internal weapon and is in orbit ready to be deployed,*" another *Guardian's* voice continued in his head.

"*We want you to go and oversee the installation and submergence of the pyramid. This time we want to avoid, if at all possible, the catastrophe that occurred on the island of the rising sun. The environment must not be altered in any way!*

To do so would be detrimental to the local inhabitants and will result in their complete elimination," stated the *Guardian.*

Chris, with his new instructions makes to turn and leave, about to make a dramatic exit himself. Let them wait on him for a change, when the voice inside his head spoke again.

"*One more thing...Each of the weapon modules for the man-made pyramids will need to be installed on a unit by unit basis. The modules are designed to fit into your ATS and are stored in this station's access bay. The first one is ready for you to deploy and is designed specifically for the Egypt pyramid,*" said the *Guardian's* voice in his head.

"*Is there anything else?*" queried *Chris*.

236

"No" came the reply, "You may go now, the Egyptian module awaits you."

"Well...that's how you know who the boss is then!" grumbled *Chris* under his breath.

"Well ok, time to get on with it! Too much is at stake!" *Chris* continued under his breath mindful of the command centre's ability to read his thoughts.

*

Chris headed to the access bay. Upon entering the *ATS* he queried if the weapons module was on board to which he received a mental image of a small rectangular black box in the cargo hold. How the *ATS* stored it was beyond him, there had appeared to be only enough space for him and him alone.

The box appears to be blinking, tiny almost imperceptible dots of light red, blue, yellow, green, sometimes white light flashed on and off randomly over the faces of the cube.

Chris and the *ATS*, now cloaked, arrived as the sun was setting over the western Egyptian horizon. The sand dust in the sky gave the setting sun a bloody sheen as if a great star born beast has been slain and its blood now covered the known galaxy. Then as if a switch had been flipped it went dark.

FIRST CONTACT

There was no moon evident in the desert sky tonight; *Chris* marvelled at the beauty of the clear night sky. The brightest stars stand out against the star peppered sky so bright they almost take the place of the absent, normally brightly shining moon. In the depths of the dry sound carrying night air, a jackal can be heard calling out for a mate, a few insects rub their hind scaly legs together making the sharp clicking noise of the what can surely only be a group of locusts.

Chris instructs the *ATS* to take him to the void inside the pyramid. Luckily the transport portal is still intact. Treasure hunters have not found the access portal...Yet!

"Surely it would not be long until they did though!"

The space in the pyramid was barely large enough for their purposes. The void is a snug fit even for the *ATS*.

In front of the *ATS* is a small rectangular space barely large enough for the cube and *Chris* to be ejected into.

"Expel Weapons Module," instructs *Chris*.

The *ATS* lifts the cube with its tube-like appendage and places it in front of the skimmer in the space provided. Projecting an image to *Chris*, the skimmer signals for him to place his hands on it. This will activate the cube and begin the construction process.

238

Two human shaped hand indentations appear on the cube's dark surface.

Chris instructs the *ATS* to expel him so he is standing in front of the cube. He places his hands on the cube at the allotted positions.

There is a faint humming and then the activity of the lights increases, the cube starts to glow; the intensity of the once tame flashing surface lights rapidly increases to a frenzy. Then with the increase in activity breaks out in a bright searing white light.

Chris, blinded by the brightness, instructs his Morph-Suit to adjust the shading in front of his retina. A moment later he receives a projection from the *ATS* stating that they must leave immediately, or risk being absorbed by the weapon module as it starts to take the required construction materials from the pyramid and build the weapon.

Chris enters the *ATS*, there is a red flashing warning that fills the embryonic sac. The weapons module is starting to drain the *ATS*'s power supply!

"*EXIT PYRAMID IMMEDIATELY!*" shouted *Chris*.

A *screeching* shriek is emitted from the *ATS*, and then they are outside the pyramid. The sun is just about to rise.

The ATS feels drained, sluggish almost drunk as it moves unsteadily around the pyramid.

239

Needing time to recover and regenerate its power supply, *Chris* instructs the *ATS* to head for Atlantis. The cloaking mechanism will not engage. So uncloaked, but unnoticed in the cover of the fading darkness, *Chris* and the *ATS* fly to the Atlantic Ocean.

There is no silky feeling no time and space that seem as one, just the humming and whirring of the *ATS* struggling to carry out his orders. Entering the chloride laden ocean, the *ATS* starts to become surer footed.

The *ATS* starts to slowly replenish its energy reserves by absorbing the required gasses and liquids from the ocean. With time it will regain a portion of its power but could never fully recharge using natural resources, no...the *ATS* could only be fully reinvigorated by the grace of the *Grand Architect*. Without the *ATS* being in full working order *Chris* himself would be at risk. He will not be able to regenerate, so not only his longevity will be threatened, but also the completion of his mission! The mission, entrusted to him by the *Grand Master*, was so important that he has no doubt the *Guardians* must have a backup plan.

He may think he is not expendable, but that would be naive! *Chris* instructed the *ATS* to head to the Atlantis pyramid, and upon reaching the access portal the pyramid allows them to enter.

Exiting the *ATS* to allow the skimmer time to regenerate, he heads to the softly glowing panels on the far side of the room. There is a table and chair next to the panels, crystal lights show him the way. Apparently, this is where he is to rest and wait until the *ATS* has recovered. The experience in the Egyptian pyramid had severely damaged the *ATS*.

It would appear that the *Guardians* have already predicted that he would be here. Their patterns of chaos predictions for the future seem to be extremely accurate, but let's hope that the weapon is not required and that the war with the *Xhoseti* back on Termite turns in mankind's favour. The pyramid weapon is only to be activated as a last resort; that is if he can succeed in his mission of uniting all Earth based human beings.

He has no doubt that the pyramid weapons will be completed and on time thanks to the *Guardians* intervention,

"Only a few thousand years are left to see if they are right though! I will continue with the other weapons modularisation when the ATS has recovered!"

With that *Chris* slumped into the chair and, lifting his feet placed them on the table.

The chair and table sense his needs and morph into a reclining memory foam chair, so comfortable that he falls into a deep, troubled sleep filled with nightmares of what will become of humanity should he fail.

*

241

EASTER ISLAND

242

Chapter Seventeen

900 AD:
Easter Island
Earth

Totu was sitting at his favourite fishing spot, testing his new hooks he had made from the shark that his father had caught last week. He didn't know what all the *fuss* was about; yes, it was a great fearsome beast from the sea, but the flesh was terrible, all rubbery and tasteless.

"*Yuk!*" he voiced his distaste.
He had to put some crab meat and salt from the sea with it just to make it palatable.

The new hooks that he had fashioned from the teeth were fantastic though; he had even cut himself a few times shaping them. The biggest issue was drilling the hole so he could thread the shark's dried gut through it for the line. Using a pointed stick and some sea sand, he had successfully managed to put a hole in each tooth. It was very tough on the hands.

All that up and down...up and down, rolling over the shaft of the stick made his hands burn. It was just like making a fire.

He threw the weighted, newly fashioned shark gut line and tooth hook into the tidal lagoon and prepared

243

to sit back and wait. He pulled the line through the fork of the sapling tree he was sitting next to.

Soon he would have to make his own fork as the tree was growing so rapidly it would be of no use to him except for shade.

The twig he had looped and tied into the gut would act as a visual aid should anything bite on the baited shark's tooth. When the twig went under the water's surface he would strike hard, pulling the gut with all his might to snare the unseen leviathan and feast on its flesh over a small fire.

"I wish for a great big fish, well a small edible one at least!" Totu said raising his hands to the sky.

For now, the twig just floated on the lagoon's surface, bobbing up and down with the ebb and flow of the small waves on the crystal-clear blue lagoon.

After a short while, enough time for him to start dozing off, the twig acting as the float, dropped sharply below the surface, catching his attention and stirring him to action. The sun's heat had made him lethargic, but no more; he grabbed the line intent on making sure that whatever had been snared didn't get away.

"Just a little more, just a little more," he murmured to himself, slowly pulling in the line and thereby taking up the slack.

FIRST CONTACT

He was just about to strike, when he heard a strange noise down at the beach. He turned to look at where the noise had emanated from.

Down on the beach there was a white haired, bearded old man just standing there. He was sure the strange looking man had not been there just a moment ago. The old man in grey, turned to look at him and smiled, white teeth flashing in the sunlight.

"Did his eyes flash as well?" Totu questioned himself, unsure of what he had just seen.

Totu looked down at his line. It had gone limp, and whatever was on the end must have slipped the hook and had got away.

"Damn!"

Hook and line forgotten, he ran down to greet the newcomer. As he got closer the man's appearance seemed to change. He became younger in appearance the closer Totu got and it was as if with every step Totu took the man grew more and more lifelike.

This stranger's clothes were very odd for this hot humid climate; he must be very hot in that grey cloak! The hair and beard, although white, were neatly trimmed and his grey eyes sparkled with life. Every few moments, as he looked around, a flash of sunlight reflected off his eyes as if there was some mother of pearl hidden in them.

245

FIRST CONTACT

XHOSETI

"Good morning young man...I have travelled a long way from the East and would like to meet with your elders. A small amount of food and water would also be most welcome. Can you take me to them?" asked *Chris* of the young local.

"Sure, mister strange man...Follow me!" spouted Totu.

"The elders will be pleased to see you if you can help with the rat problem we are having on the island," turning to walk inland, shark hooks forgotten, Totu led *Chris* towards the village.

While they walk, *Chris* notices some large headed statues lined up on a stone platform; there are more scattered around the island. Some of them stand ten metres tall and have ceremonial red hats. He turned to Totu to enquire about these strange statues, asking what they were for and who had built them.

"They are the statues of the space gods. The space gods came down from the stars to visit us a long time ago.

"They wanted to know how many men we were and to see if we could make any statues. They showed our ancestors how to make tools to cut the rock, use logs to roll the stones to places that they had determined. Then they taught us how to shape the stone with fire and water. To finish off the great statues, they then showed us how to take the sand

246

FIRST CONTACT

from the beach and rub the giant statues smooth. We also used the sand to hollow out the eye sockets of the Moai.

The Moai, yes that is what we call them, are carved to resemble the star gods," explained Totu.

"They look remarkably like bigger versions of the Guardians back on the orbiting station," thought *Chris*.

"Looks like the *Guardians* have been performing some kind of survey on the island's population and capabilities! So that's why they prefabricated the pyramid for this location! The population must not have been large enough, nor the resources available to build the pyramid!" muttered *Chris* under his breath, making sure he was not heard by his new-found companion.

Chris could see no large animals that could be harnessed for pulling the huge megalithic stones that would be required for the building of the island's pyramid. Manpower was all that was available and there just was not enough of it!

They continued for another thirty minutes and then came to the village. It was primitive even by Roman standards, merely stone and rectangular shaped mud brick huts with interwoven leaf mat sheets for the roof. He could see a total of ten large huts. Outside most of them there were women sitting on make shift stools, some with babies strapped to their backs, others

247

FIRST CONTACT

fanning themselves with leaf mats to stave off the heat and humidity. Those without the mats seemed oblivious to the flies hovering or crawling around their bodies and faces.

The rest of the villagers, men, children, seemed to be virtually naked. A small loin cloth, barely covering the essentials, appeared to have been donned for modesty's sake only.

Again, he can understand why the *Guardians* chose to prefabricate this pyramid.

Chris was led to a hut with no particular differences to any of the others. Inside is a large man sitting on a chair also wearing very little, just like the other villagers. The only sign of his importance is a feathered hat on his head and a few ornaments. Brass bangles adorn his wrists and ankles. He gestured for *Chris* to sit on the woven mat provided.

Chris sat, crossing his legs and waited for the village chief (he presumed), to speak. Soon six other members of the village enter the hut, three male, three female. Each have similar brass bands on wrists and ankles but no feathered headdress.

Chris seemed to be positioned in the centre of this elder's council. It seems to be a common theme for him when he must interact with a council, strange how his new hosts seem to be following the ways of the *Guardians*!

248

Still he waits, knowing that his hosts will inform him when they wish to interact with him.

One of the female elders produces a bowl of clear liquid; she takes a sip and passes the bowl around the sitting figures. The bowl is passed to the head chief last of all. He takes a sip and then passes the bowl to *Chris*.

Chris mimics the council and takes a sip; a warm fire burns his throat as he swallows.

"This must be the local intoxication brew!" he thought to himself. His modified genetics and Morph-Suit can safely filter out any unwanted toxins.

After the ceremonial drink, the Chief signalled that he wished to speak. The other council members signify that he is to continue by raising their hands, palms flat and facing upward to the sky.

"I am Ranu, the head chief of Easter Island. We welcome you to our humble village. Being isolated by the sea, we do not get many visitors! How are you called stranger?"

"Thank you Ranu. Chief of Easter Island. I am called *Chris* of the East. I have travelled a great distance from the East to bring you a grave warning of an impending doom!"

There was a tense silence. Then all the elders started talking amongst themselves. The smell of panic and fear filled the air as the tempo of their voices increased to one of near hysteria.

249

FIRST CONTACT

"*Silence* my fellow elders; what this stranger tells us of is the end of the world. The star gods foretold this to us and we have known the time would come, just not when. *Now we know!*

Tell me stranger *Chris*, when will this doom come and what must we do to avert it?" asked Ranu.

"How long will it take you to build great sailing boats to carry all of your people to the eastern land of Chile? Chile is a land which lies many months sailing away in the far East," explained *Chris*.

"This is the only way you can save your people! If I am correct you will only have three months or one season from planting a crop to harvesting it before you must leave this island," *Chris* continued.

A pin dropping could have been heard in the silence that followed. *Chris* decided to change the subject,

"Now Ranu, Chief of Easter Island...tell me of the rat problem that plagues your people."

Chief Ranu, initially taken aback at this stranger's knowledge of their rat problem, goes on to explain that they have been infested with these large two-foot-long, rodents.

"They eat the roots of the young shrubs and trees; all the bird's eggs are either eaten or destroyed by the rats. Eventually the rats will kill off everything, both plant and animal!" the Chief paused before continuing,

250

"They breed constantly, but for every two we kill to eat, three appear in their place. They are a great source of food, but the rats are winning the numbers game and now our boat building resources are being diminished by the rat's efforts!"

Chris listens to Ranu with concern. If the rats destroy all the trees, then the people of Easter Island will not be able to get off it before the pyramid is to be submerged!

He does not want any casualties, nor for that matter any witnesses when they submerge the pyramid. Besides, the *Guardians* have interfered with these people way too much already. They will of course be able to justify their actions even though they are interfering with his plans.

"Regarding the rat infestation problem, I would recommend a rat cull! You should organise your people and arm each of the able-bodied men and women with a wooden beating stick. Find a shallow sinkhole, no more than ten meters deep. Send your men down into it to find any exits and block them up. Only use stones large enough so that the rats will not be able to escape the trap!

Gather as much of the fuel that you use to make your torches burn into pots and take them to the top of the sinkhole.

251

Throw food into the hole and then wait for the rats to come. When sufficient rats have entered the hole, pour the oil down the walls of the hole and light it. Any escaping rats you must club to death with the beating sticks.

Make sure the sinkholes are near to where the rats have been seen. If you have to dig some then do it. Do this as many times as required to get rid of the rodent problem."

"Thank you, stranger *Chris*. That sounds like a good plan," replied Ranu, a slight slur in his speech.

"I will arrange for the villagers to start gathering the food and to go and get the fuel from the tar pit. It is on the far side of the island. We will fill as many bowls as we can gather with the tar." continued Ranu.

Within a week, the rats have been dealt with and the sound of trees being chopped down could be heard ringing in the forest.

Chris and the head boat builder drew up the plans for the new boats. Ranu was left organising food stocks, rodent drying taking up a large part of his time. The food baskets were filled with the rats that escaped the fires and soon the fish stocks were also filling up, thanks to Totu's new shark tooth hooks.

Within a month, the forests were bare, not a mature tree stood. The dried fish and rat stocks are for the villagers to live off during the two-month journey to the East. All the yams and other edible tubers have been dug up, all the fruit picked and dried.

They were almost ready.

The storage baskets were as full as they would ever get. The goats are to be taken with them to provide fresh milk and when the animals' feed runs out, they will be slaughtered to provide fresh meat.

Water would be the biggest issue! They could not simply rely on the rain over the ocean to stop them dying of thirst.

"How to keep the stores they had gathered from going stagnate and becoming undrinkable?" pondered *Chris*.

They could only take enough water for two, maybe three weeks. After that the water stocks would either be consumed or undrinkable.

Ranu came up with an ingenious method of distilling sea water.

Each boat had a clay bowl with sides high enough so that the blowing wind would not affect the fire deep down inside. A mixture of tar and wood could be burnt inside it, giving them some control over the heat produced. The burning bowl was large enough to place the specially manufactured clay jar in it, the lid of which had a tubular spout that protruded past the bowl's edge and pointed downwards.

253

Sea water would be placed in the clay jar that was then to be heated. This spout would then be used to gather the water vapour from the heated jar. This may not produce a huge amount of water, but at least what was collected would be drinkable. They only needed to take enough of the tar, wood and flint to last the two-month journey east to Chile.

*

When it was time to leave the island, Ranu expressed his concern that *Chris* was not coming with them. *Chris* replied that he had his own boat in one of the tidal caves below the cliff and took Ranu to see his own small wooden ship that the *ATS* had morphed into.

Without celebration or fanfare, Ranu and his entire Easter Island people boarded the boats and with a few waves and cheers set sail for Chile.

"Good! That's one disaster averted," thought *Chris*, *"Now for the pyramid!"*

Entering the *ATS*, *Chris* sent a message to the *Guardians* that they could begin the ascent of the pyramid scheduled for this region.

A few days later a reddish orange ball of fire streaked down from the heavens heading for his position.

*

FIRST CONTACT

Ranu, sitting on the stern of his boat was looking up at the sky enjoying a bit of dried rat and washing it down with a bowl of his private fire water stock, when he saw the flames in the sky heading straight for the island they had once called home. He hoped that *Chris,* the stranger, was far, far away from the flaming ball of the sky.

"Thank you, Chris, for warning us of the end of the world! Soon we will be in a new land; much will need to be done. A new village will need to be built, food and water sourced. What of the local tribes? Will they accept us or fight us?" he gulped down some more of the bowls fiery contents trying not to worry too much about the future just yet!

*

The pyramid still cloaked hung five metres above the sea three kilometres from the east shores of Easter Island. Inside the pyramid *Chris* was inspecting the panels of the weapon; all appeared to be in order. Now he had only to wait for the right time to begin the submergence.

"Ranu and his people must be nearing their destination within the week!" thought *Chris.*

He can issue the order to descend then.

By the end of the week a tropical storm had formed to the South of his position and was heading straight

255

towards the island. He will hold off with the descent until absolutely necessary to give Ranu and his people a better chance should anything go wrong.

The storm arrived sooner than anticipated! The pyramid shifted and swung in the increasingly strengthening storm.

Inside the pyramid *Chris* was getting ready to enter the *ATS*. The descent and subsequent submergence will need to start within the next thirty minutes or the pyramid may fall from the sky and into the sea.

At the moment, just keeping the pyramid in place was causing a huge strain on the central energy crystal. The energy requirements were so great that the crystal was being drained faster than the kinetic regenerator mechanisms could replenish its power. A red warning light fired in his mind and at the same time the panel lit up. He must give the command to submerge now or risk damaging the pyramid!

Entering the *ATS* he instructed the skimmer to exit the pyramid. He then gave the command for the pyramid to descend into the ocean.

The pyramid started to move down towards the sea. All was proceeding as expected when a freak wave hit the side of the pyramid tilting it a few degrees to the vertical. The drain on the central crystal is increased and just for a moment the pyramid drops a few meters, and then falls into the ocean. The

256

antigravity motors inside the pyramid scream as they struggle to slow the descent of the pyramid, eventually gaining control, but it's too late!

The resulting tsunami wave is enormous!

Above the descending pyramid, *Chris* looks on in horror as the pyramid falls into the ocean.

"Thank goodness the islanders have been evacuated. If they were here they would have all been killed," thought *Chris*.

The tsunami wave completely overran the island destroying everything in its path. Nothing was left alive.

No trees, shrubs or grassland remained on the island. No insects, bird or reptile were to be seen. Those fortunate enough to fly away had already headed westward. Incredibly some of the moa statues were still standing. Others lay on their backs, white eyes staring up at the sky!

"Why had this great catastrophe been allowed to happen!" their eyes seemed to question of the sky gods whom they were meant to represent.

Chris, checking if the pyramid had survived the almost disastrous recent happenings, received the all clear as far as the weapon was concerned. The only damage seemed to be to the access portal. This seemed to be the weak point in the *Guardian's* design,

257

but there was nothing to be done about it now. He would not be entering this pyramid through that portal now or anytime in the future. At least the weapon was safe though!

"Only one left!"

He can feel the glare of his mother's eyes on the back of his head. In his mind he sees her scowling at him, arms folded. He needs to be more careful in the future!

"Now to get back to the Guardian's station. Time to get the China pyramid's weapon working," *Chris* said out loud as much to reassure himself as his parents.

With that he instructed the *ATS* to take him back to the orbiting station, where he was sure a reprimand was awaiting him.

Time and space seem as one, that welcome silky feeling... and then he was docking with the *Guardian's* orbiting station.

*

ROBERT J STEPHENS

VIKINGS

FIRST CONTACT

Chapter Eighteen

1000 AD:
Earth
Scandinavia

Elrige stirred from his animal skin covered bed. His wife still sleeps peacefully beside him. He smiles down at her, remembering the dancing and feasting of last night. He leaves her to sleep, *"Sleep well my vixen!"* he whispered to himself.

Grabbing his fur overcoat, he picked up his axe and slowly drew back the bed chamber flap. The noise that woke him appeared to be coming from outside the great hall. There is a clang of steel on steel, some hushed words and then silence.

He creeps to the first of the sleeping lumps lying on the floor of the great hall making as little noise as possible. Putting his hand over the slumbering man's mouth, he wakes him and puts a finger to his own lips indicating for him to keep quiet.

Once the man was awake, he moved to the next sleeping figure and rouses him with the same technique. After a few minutes most of his men are awake. They are alert and have their weapons ready, if not their armour. If possible, they will need to get their shields as well, who knows what the next few minutes will bring...

One thing's for certain, those armoured men outside meant them no good. It is then that he smelt the burning wood.

They have set his hall on fire!

Elrige and his men must decide. Burn in here or die out there! The men look to him for instruction,

"See you in Valhalla!" whispered Elrige to them and with that storms the hall's wooden doors. He bounces off them as they are thick and strong, he should know, he helped his *father* install them,

"THE DOORS ARE BARRED!

HELP ME CHOP THROUGH THEM...

AS SOON AS WE BREACH THEM...COVER US WITH SHIELDS.

The cowards, whoever they are will be waiting arrows drawn! They are hoping to keep us inside long enough so the smoke overcomes us and then break in, saving the women for their own uses and the children to be sold to the Arabs in Southern Spain," explained Elrige, the rage in his eyes starting to flame and burn with an intensity worthy of Odin's forge.

Well they won't have it that easy with him and his men! They were all battle hardened, having been blooded in their raids on the North of England.

With the first raids on England, they had experienced little or no resistance from the English

Kings, but as the raids became more frequent the English became more organised.

On the previous raid he had lost five men. The Valkyrie will have taken them straight to Odin's great hall to feast and drink forever as they had fought well and died like real heroes of old.

Then the doors burst open, and an arrow hits Elrige in the shoulder before his men's shields can close around him. In an instant they are encircled by a half moon of Stonghelm's men.

The coward! Even though they have a feud, this is no way to solve things, like a thief in the night!

"WHEN I TAKE YOUR HEAD STRONGHELM...THERE WILL BE NO VALHALLA FOR YOU...YOU COWARDLY SHIT!" shouted Elrige, his voice hoarse from the smoke.

The red haze of battle descends over his eyes and he rushes past the shield wall, ripping the arrow from his shoulder. He swings his axe, tearing into the would-be murderers. In his other hand he holds a knife which he uses in a slashing motion, removing the intestines of the man closest to him.

To Elrige the battle is all a bloody haze!

His men, having seen him go berserk before, stay out of the way. They simply stand back and watch him destroy all those who stand in his path.

A few of his men, instead of watching Elrige go berserk, start to throw sand and snow over the flaming

262

hall trying to douse the flames. The rest watch Elrige. He was like a fire that was always smouldering, then with a whoosh, like the oil from the pine tree cones when they catch fire, roar in a blaze of extreme heat then die just as suddenly.

Blood soaked and bleeding from gashes on his legs and torso, Elrige held the severed head of Stronghelm above his head and let out an animal like roar. With that he collapsed to his knees, spent and exhausted. He then fell face first into the snow.

Two of his men rush to pick him up and carry him into the now smouldering hall. They need to dress his wounds quickly while he still has the fire in his belly. To leave the wounds would mean infection and that is no way for a great warrior to die, bed ridden and covered in stinking maggots.

Some of the women, awakened by the noise, come out from behind their respective chamber flaps.

One of them stokes the fire in the centre of hall and puts on the pot, filling it with water. An older woman adds some herbs that she had previously gathered from the nearby forest. She gets out her fishing gut and a bone needle.

The men bring Elrige towards the fire and lay him down in front of her. He looks like he is possessed; his blue eyes have dark pupils, wide and confrontational, glaring at everyone. It is as if he is already in Valhalla.

263

The old lady takes a rag and dips it in the now boiling water; she wipes the blood from around his wounds, then takes more herbs from a bag on her shoulder and puts some in her mouth, chews them a few times and gulps some mead from a nearby gourd hanging on the wall.

Removing the saliva and mead covered herbs from her mouth; she places them in Elrige's wounds. Taking the needle and gut she stitches up his wounds one at a time, leaving a fingers width between each stitch. The gap is to let out the demon spirits and the pus that will surely come over the next few days!

Once the pus has stopped, she will remove the herb poultices and stitch the rest of the wound closed.

A few days later Elrige, having drunk from one of the old hag's broths, awoke from this drug induced sleep. He had a vague recollection of what took place, most of it a red blurry haze. Getting up he put on his bear skin hide and stumbled outside.

There he sees the coward Stronghelm's head on a stick. The ravens have already pecked out his eyes and torn off his nose and ears. The rest of the bodies of Stronghelm's cowardly followers are piled in a heap ready for him to light in the funeral pyre. They will not be in Odin's hall but still they were Vikings and as such will be cremated. This will also keep the wolves at bay as they will soon smell the rotting carcasses and want to take their share!

Taking the already lit torch, he threw it onto the pine tree logs beneath the bodies. It took a few minutes before the oil of the pine tree sap caught but soon the flames started to crackle and spit.

The smell of pine oil and burning human flesh fills the air, making some of his men drool. He turned to look at each one of them, those with the evil thoughts in their minds drop their eyes to the ground trying to hide their secret, but he now knows who they are!

*

Chris, having aided the Romans' conversion, had witnessed the rise of Christianity during Constantine's Roman rule. Within a few centuries all of the Roman Empire had been converted to Christianity.

The battle between Christianity and Muslimism had been raging for centuries in lower Europe and Northern Africa; not all was going the Christians way though! The Roman Empire was slowly changing from Christian to Muslim in upper Africa. Egypt, once Christian from the late first century had become Muslim in the mid seventh century.

The same trend took place for most of the other Roman African provinces.

265

XHOSETI

Britain on the other hand remained Christian. Being isolated via the seas it had remained so without threat and is now ruled by the Christian King Ethelred.

Many of the northern European countries had already been converted to Christianity; only the Vikings of Scandinavia still believe in the old gods. *Chris* must do something about that.

Time is running out and there is still so much to do before the Xhoseti threat becomes a reality. The more religions who believe in a single deity the better!

Mankind must be united at all costs!

Unfortunately, diversity is the key to life!

Not all can agree who is right or, for that matter, wrong; tolerance and acceptance is imperative. If there are three major religions, his task to coordinate mankind against the *Xhoseti* when they arrive will be so much easier.

*

Elrige consults with his subjects...

"There is a problem!"

Raids by the Viking warlords against each other are becoming more and more frequent.

"The raid by Stronghelm last week is proof that we as Vikings are expanding beyond the limit of our resources. Children and women go hungry every day,

266

especially when the winter months come. Every year each lord must take more and more drastic steps to ensure his clan survives! The only way to do that is to fight each other," explained Elrige.

"It must be the influence of these Christian Churches to the South; they sow dissension amongst us. We, the true believers in Valhalla and the old gods, must stand against the Christians. May Loki play with them and send them all to the abyss!" snarled Elrige.

"We all know that the Christian land of England to the Southwest has great lands to plough and wealth to plunder. If we stay here, all we have to look forward to is more of the same, and as the wise man often says, doing the same thing repeatedly and expecting a different result is the providence of fools. *So...what say you, shall we relocate to the rich land of England?"*

There were a few shakes of the head, a few mumbles concerning the will of the true gods and let Loki have the Christians...Odin will send a sign...The grumbling continued for some time...

Eventually, one of Elrige's men got to his feet to raise his concern, "The old gods will desert us if we go to that Christian land, what about the women and children, what about our cattle?" the group mumbled agreement and the grumbling continues.

FIRST CONTACT

XHOSETJ

"Enough! We take the women and children, kill the cattle, dry the meat, gather the harvest, and move on to a new life in England!

Come spring we will plant crops...build longboats to take us to England and then, with the end of summer, reap the crops, dry the meat and move on.

That is my ruling!

If there are any who wish to stay here, stand and say so now. There will be no reprisals or judgements. *Who is not with me?"*

Some murmur and curse under their heavy beards quietly to themselves, but no one stands to disagree.

"Good...then it's settled. To England in the autumn."

*

Come autumn, six longboats leave the shores of Scandinavia heading south-westward to the green hills of Northumbria in England.

The sea trip was uneventful, a few high waves from some light storms, but thanks to the skill of the Norsemen who had sailed these seas before, the journey was taken in its stride. They ride the waves as one would ride a young gelding horse. Luck and bravery making up for a lack of skill on the odd occasion when some of the longboats looked sure to

FIRST CONTACT

capsize. Soon they land on the beaches of Northumbria, England!

The only thing that plagues Elrige is the repeated dream he kept on experiencing.

He is standing next to a great oak tree, the branches gnarled and twisted. It seems so ancient as it groans in the wind. With every breath he takes, the tree takes one too. A large dangling shape catches his attention, his vision blurs, and he is standing next to the hanging man.

He has a great beard and horned helmet; a patch covers his one eye. His face is blue from the tightness of the rope around his neck. In his hand he holds a great double-sided axe, black blood drips from it!

His eye opens; he stares at Elrige and then points to Elrige's left shoulder. Elrige turns to see what Odin is pointing at. Standing there, wearing all green shining scale like armour, is the god Loki, his great curved horned helmet ringed with gold straps, steam rising from the top of the pointed horns.

Elrige stands transfixed! Loki, grinning and then looking Elrige straight in the eyes, raises his spear and stabs Odin in the side. Leaves spring from the wound, then earth and worms. He always wakes at this point in the dream, sweat pouring from his forehead. He is always wet with sweat under his bear skin cover.

*

FIRST CONTACT

Immediately upon landing Elrige sends out scouts. The scouts return with some Viking warriors from the local settlement which is ruled by the Viking King Forkbeard.

Elrige, caught off guard, goes with ten of his finest warriors to meet the settlement's king. When he arrives, Elrige takes note of the establishment. The settlement has a wooded spiked defence wall; the land around the walls had been cleared of all trees and shrubbery. A dry moat like trench has been dug around the fortified settlement. Two large high gates stand ajar, with a wooden ramp extended over the land moat. It looks like it can be drawn back behind the walls with ropes and pulleys.

To Elrige's warrior eye it looks like such a place could be easily defended. It's only weakness would be an attack from fire arrows, that is, if they do not have a source of water to douse the flames.

He follows Forkbeard's men into the settlement and passes a stone rimmed water well in the centre of the square. To either side of the square are men and women going about their business. A blacksmith strikes some glowing steel, making what appears to be a horse shoe while the horse stands idly by eating a bag of oats.

There are shield and armour makers, a tannery and a market selling fresh farm produce. Thatched rectangular shaped wooden huts are laid out row by

270

row in an orderly manner; they go on as far as Elrige could see. There must be enough housing here for hundreds of men and women. All appear to be in good health!

At the far end of the square is the great hall, a massive building, built with huge wooden logs for the walls and main columns, then thatched with local reed for the roof. The group stops in front of the great hall and dismounts.

"*King* Forkbeard will see you now! No weapons are allowed inside; only the King's guard will have weapons. Do not try anything. You are here under the protection of the King and as such you are safe within these walls," one of the dismounted armed men explained to Elrige.

Grudgingly leaving his weapons behind, Elrige signals for his men to remain outside, as he entered the building.

Light streams in from the roof through raised ramps held open by wooden struts that are attached to a rope and a pulley system. The central fire smoke rises up and out of the building through these openings in the roof.

King Forkbeard readjusts his position on his not so comfortable high chair. The wooden chair groans under his great bulk. He gestures for Elrige to come closer.

271

FIRST CONTACT

"My eyesight is not as good as it once was," explains Forkbeard, "I have no sons and my strength is failing. If you prove worthy, for it is no coincidence that you arrive when Odin is looking to take me to his banqueting hall, all this can be yours. How many men do you command?" Forkbeard's raspy voice indicates just how sick he really is. A chesty dry rattle emanates from his chest every time he draws a breath.

"I have six longboats filled with warriors, old men, women and children. My warriors are all battle hardened and number around forty," answered Elrige.

"Good...good; that will give us the advantage over that dog, Kriger. That is if you wish to join us!

I offer my hand to you and yours in friendship and with an alliance between us, Kriger will surely not attack. There is enough here for everyone in this green and fertile land. There is no need for us to squabble amongst ourselves. *We need to join forces to attack those Christian dogs in the South!"*

"Thank you for your offer, we are strangers here and with your openness and friendship to us, we will accept your shelter and in return offer our fealty to your rule. I will go to tell my men the good news and return by nightfall."

"Good Elrige, hurry now as I fear that Kriger will be upon us before three sunsets have passed. With you here behind my walls he will have to parley."

272

With that Elrige set off with his men to tell those waiting down by the shoreline the good news.

*

Chris, taking on the role of a Christian priest, has been an advisor to King Ethelred for the past six months. The castle walls have been rebuilt at *Chris's* advice and now have an earthen rubble and sand wall encased with locally quarried stones instead of just a stone wall. This will ensure that any attack by ballista will be absorbed by the earthen structure.

The moat has been drained and wooden pikes have been placed facing to the heavens for any would be attackers falling off the retractable bridge should that situation arise. When the moat is refilled, the spikes will be barely visible.

"My lord, the heathen Norsemen have landed again in Northumbria. Their numbers are getting greater by the day. You must ride out to meet them and destroy or convert them to Christianity," *Chris* advised the King.

"And how do you propose to do that? My men are well armed and armoured, but they are inexperienced in the art of open warfare. Behind our high walls we are safe! Why not let them run around burning and looting, it stops them looking South to our borders!" replied the King.

273

"Soon my lord, they will turn their attention southwards and you must be ready. Build a greater army than theirs. The Viking are only a few thousand at the moment and that is only should they all co-operate. You can order ten times that number. Convert or kill them!"

The King sat down on one of the church pews and then going down on his knees he bent his head in prayer asking God what to do. *Chris* turned and left the church and the King to his prayers.

"This King will need some more convincing. Time to visit his dreams! What scenario to send, power maybe, history maker? Now that's the way to deal with this King."

Chris prepared for what plan of action he will take tonight.

Later that night...cloaked, Chris waited in the King's chamber. The King sleeps alone. After draining his goblet of diluted wine, he disrobes, uses the chamber pot, and gets into bed. Soon the King was snoring peacefully.

It was then that *Chris* enters Ethelred's dreams as a cloaked white haired and bearded old man,

"Build an army worthy of the King of Legend that you are...
History will remember you for converting the last of the heathen Norsemen to the Christian faith...

274

Build as many boats as you need...Then sail them North with your fleet while sending your ground troops on the land northward to meet and convert or slay the Norsemen. Attack them from the South and the North so they have to fight on two fronts."

Task done and still cloaked, *Chris* left the room and closed the door behind him, hoping that his work here will be fruitful.

*

With his followers safely behind the walls of Forkbeard's settlement, Elrige discusses his plans to invade Wessex before winter sets in. It's a risky strategy but if they are successful all will be well fed for the harsh winter to come.

He only needed Kriger to join them.

The following day, the challenge is made.
Kriger wants Forkbeard to surrender or fight! He has more men than Forkbeard and as such has the advantage. His spies have not yet found out that Elrige has joined Forkbeard's army.

"Let me ride out and meet him, I think I can get him to join our fight against the English," with a nod from Forkbeard, Elrige exits the hall, mounts his horse and rides out to meet the awaiting enemy army.

"Who are you?" shouted Kriger.

275

"I am recently joined with the Forkbeard clan and as such represent them. I have a proposal that may be to your liking. What say you to an alliance against the weak and spineless English of Wessex? We will share the spoils between the three of us. If we fail, Odin will welcome us as great heroes. Our names will go down in history as the greatest of the Norsemen this side of the sea!"

Kriger is silent; his spies have not done their jobs. He will have to remove a few eyes and ears as they have not been using them very well. Kriger, not a man to miss an opportunity, mulled this proposal over in his mind. What's to lose? *Greatness, war, women, plunder and treasure. Ok, he's in!*

"Let us meet and discuss our plans, I will erect a meeting place here in the field. Bring Forkbeard."

With that Elrige started back to Forkbeard's settlement.

Walking in to the great hall, he sees Forkbeard slumped in his chair; a few men and women gathered around him.

"The King is dead!" proclaims one of the men, turning to Elrige, "Before Odin took him, Forkbeard wished that you would sit upon his throne and take his place as he has no rightful heir. *You see he was sterile!*

Do you accept this great honour?" Elrige, knees trembling slightly, replied, "I will take this great honour

276

bestowed upon me and be the warrior King that you all expect me to be."

"*LONG LIVE THE KING...LONG LIVE THE KING,*" the men and women in the great hall shout.

Taking the crown from Forkbeards head, he ordered the funeral pyre to be built in the centre of the square.

"Now to deal with Kriger!" said Elrige.
Crown on head, King Elrige rides out to meet Kriger, twenty warriors in tow.

Kriger upon hearing of the death of his adversary shouts, phlegm spraying from his mouth,

"*WHAT?*

You expect me to accept you, an unknown pup, as King? That is a right that can only be earnt in blood!

I CHALLENGE YOU FOR THE CROWN IN SINGLE COMBAT. DO YOU ACCEPT...OR WILL YOU SUBMIT TO ME AS YOUR RIGHTFUL KING?"

Elrige has no choice; to have travelled over the sea risking everything just to submit to this tyrant would betray his people, never mind the gods.

Accepting the challenge, the warriors form a circle of twenty men, half his, half Kriger's.

No shields, axes only, the men square up to each other. Elrige tears off his shirt, foam leaking from his mouth and starts toward Kriger.

277

Kriger, seeing the blood crazed berserker heading towards him, began to have second thoughts. He has heard of these men who are vassals of the gods, not being used to the confines of a mortal's body, the god drives the recipient mad, they fear nothing and feel no pain, no wounds can stop them, *the only way to defeat a berserker is to chop his head off!*

"So be it!" thought Kriger and charged.

The battle is over in minutes, Elrige emerges victorious, blood covering his face and torso, still foaming at the mouth he raises the head of Kriger above his head and shouts,

"IS THERE ANY ONE ELSE... IS THERE ANY ONE ELSE WHO WOULD BE KING?"

As one, all parties kneel before the King of the Norsemen over the sea.

"KING ELRIGE...WE SALUTE YOU...MAY ODIN GIVE YOU WISDOM AND THOR GIVE YOU STRENGTH!" came the roar from those present.

*

Commander James shifted his weight from his right to his left hip, not used to this amount of time in the saddle. He cursed again, as yet another blister popped and oozed fluid down the inside of his thigh. Damn these Norsemen and their pagan ways. Still, after this it's back to Bessie and the Ale & Mugg back in his home town, that is of course dependant on if he returns from this little stab and thrust scuffle.

He has heard horrific tales of the Viking's brutality. Alfred is with the ships that are to land in the North and attack these bastards from behind while he takes them upfront. The scouts tell him that they have around five thousand men. His own men number twice that and still another five thousand Englishmen will bear down on them from behind when they land.

The scouts have returned.

"At last!" thought James, *"Time to wipe out these heathen bastards."*

"My lord, the Vikings are encamped on the next hill, they have the high ground and are sending a party to discuss terms tomorrow morning. Looks like they will surrender! *Must be our larger army...surely that has put the fear of God into them!"* the returning scout informed Commander James.

"Right! All halt and set up camp here, start clearing the trees for wood, I want fires burning the whole night. Get the horses fed and issue the rations. Make sure everyone is well fed. No ale though, I want everyone to be alert! Tomorrow we will decide the fate of all England and Christianity," commanded James.

With that Commander James's orders are issued and carried out with military precision. Soon the air

279

was filled with the sound of axes being blunted on wood, the smell and sight of wet burning wood filled the air, tear inducing smoke fills the makeshift campsite.

Groups of men cluster around the fires, having eaten their rations, a bit of dried meat and half a loaf of bread. Some of the younger, less experienced soldiers speculate about tomorrow's battle, some with feverish excitement, others try not to show their fear. The older, more experienced solders try to think of nothing more than how to stay at the back of the army. Let the young eager ones run into those Viking blades, dull them a bit; weaken the flesh and resolve of the enemy with their superior numbers. *Survival is the key here, not glory!*

As the night deepens, fires burn low, men doze, some fitfully, others enjoy the sleep of babes, secure in the thought that the Viking surrender in the morning would ensure that they would soon be on their way back to wives and families.

It was then the Vikings attacked!
Flames and screams filled the air!

Commander James had been waiting for just such an attack to start. Using his slumbering men as bait, he has hundreds of his finest men in full battle attire waiting out of sight under cover in the tents; a trap has been set for these Viking heathens. His sentry eyes and spies had informed him as soon as the Vikings entered the encampment. The trap was sprung, a few of his men lost their lives, but the fifty or so Viking raiders were quickly rounded up and put to the sword or made to surrender.

He took five of the survivors, stripped them naked and sent them scurrying back to their new King Elrige, let them tell him of the vast number of men he commands,

"Tell your pagan King, that the Christian King Ethelred sends his own demands, surrender or convert to Christianity, those are the terms and there can only be one outcome tomorrow!" said Commander James to the five men before he let them go.

*

On hearing the news from his returning men, Elrige flew into a rage,

"May Thor bring his mighty hammer down on this ant of a commander; I will eat his heart myself if that is what Odin wills."

The following day, both sides test each other's defences. The English archers cannot pierce the shield wall from the low lying plain and the Vikings charges are halted by the pike men under James's command. The battle is at best a stalemate. The high ground of

Elrige makes all the difference when it comes to the numbers game.

The next day, when Alfred's men attack the Vikings from behind, the battle is all but over. With the setting of the sun, less than three thousand Vikings are left. The English have fared far worse and have lost double the men that the Vikings have. Both sides are determined to fight on though.

*

Chris, having been a passive bystander in this battle, felt that the time was right for him to visit Elrige. He will do so this evening. A push in the right direction could end this battle and unite all of England, another step towards mankind's civilisation and unification.

Elrige was taking council with what was left of his warrior shield chiefs,
"How are we to defeat such a vast amount of men, for every man I kill, two more take their place. It is as if Thor and Odin have deserted us!" this from a berserker was grim news indeed. His men feel the lack of confidence emanating from Elrige with each word he speaks,
"What manner of gods do these English pray to?" frustration edging Elrige's words.

One of his shield chiefs stood up and indicated that he wished to speak. Elrige sits and gives him the floor.

"I am no great berserker warrior like you King Elrige, but I have many summers under my belt. I speak only from rumour and whispers, but the English are united by their worship of one God. How else can they have gathered such numbers? They believe that their one God is on their side and that they can only win! It sure looks like they will win the battle, maybe not tomorrow or even the next, but eventually. Perhaps it is time to leave the old gods behind, they belong across the sea. The God here is too strong!"

There is some nodding of heads, a few shake their heads in disagreement, but overall cohesion is not what resides around this war council table. Tomorrow will be the decider, all or nothing.

That night, *Chris* cloaked, entered Elrige's tent. The Viking King is snoring...loudly; his two guards have also nodded off, too much mead...and are asleep at their posts.

Projecting into Elrige's head,

"Elrige, I come to you in this form, to warn you of the demise of the old ways and gods. While you have been at war in Middle Earth, so have we here in Asgard. Loki...that treacherous little imp of a god has finally betrayed us all. There was a great battle, only Thor and I remain. All other Guardians have been slain! So, it is

283

with a heavy heart and mind that we are not as strong or united as we once were. I give you leave to worship the new Christian God. It would be to all Viking's benefit to make peace with the English and you should be the first to be baptised. Together you can forge a new better life for all under your command as a Christian!"

With that seed planted, *Chris* left the tent and returned to King Ethelred. Another man's dreams must be influenced to ensure that the surrender, if offered, is accepted without egos and honours being bruised.

*

Within the week, all of England is ruled by King Ethelred and over the next decade, the majority of Europe and Britain is Christian.

Progress is really gathering speed!

Chris, satisfied, entered the *ATS* to regenerate.

Little did *Chris* realise that a united Europe all under Christianity would only bring more blood and carnage in the centuries to come.

Man's thirst for conflict will never be satisfied!

"*Deepest part of the Atlantic Ocean. Find the pyramid and take me there. I feel exhausted.*

I need to rest.

Wake me if there is an emergency or if instructed by the Guardians," Chris instructed the *ATS,* slipping into stasis as the *ATS* released melatonin into his blood stream.

Time and space appear as one... that familiar silky feeling and then *darkness* as *Chris* slipped into hibernation to wait for the time that he will be called upon once again by the *Guardians.*

***

FJRST CONTACT

XHOSETI

Acknowledgements:

I would like to thank my father John Stephens for the inspiration of the seven tribes' way back in my youth.

To Jackie Stephens for correcting my grammar, which was never a strong point!

Most of all I wish to thank my wife, Mandy Stephens for her patience and input. And for her support and inspiration to write the *Xhoseti* series.

*

pentopublish2018

FIRST CONTACT

Printed in Poland
by Amazon Fulfillment
Poland Sp. z o.o., Wrocław